TRIBES

TRIBES

ARTHUR SLADE

WENDY
LAMB
BOOKS

Published by
Wendy Lamb Books
an imprint of
Random House Children's Books
a division of Random House, Inc.
1540 Broadway
New York, New York 10036

Visit us on the Web! www.randomhouse.com/teens
Educators and librarians, for a variety of teaching tools, visit us at
www.randomhouse.com/teachers

Library of Congress Cataloging-in-Publication Data

Slade, Arthur G. (Arthur Gregory)
   Tribes / Arthur Slade.
     p. cm.
Summary: For Percy, the loss of his father and the death of his best friend
build to a head during the last week before high school graduation.
    ISBN 0-385-73003-9 (trade)
  [1. High schools—Fiction. 2. Schools—Fiction. 3. Cliques
(Sociology)—Fiction. 4. Suicide—Fiction. 5. Anthropology—Fiction.
6. Self-mutilation—Fiction. 7. Saskatoon (Sask.)—Fiction.
8. Canada—Fiction.] I. Title.
PZ7.S628835 Tr 2002
[Fic]—dc21

2002000018

The text of this book is set in 12-point Optima.

Book design by Melissa J Knight

Manufactured in the United States of America

September 2002

10   9   8   7   6   5   4   3   2   1
BVG

For Scott Treimel, who believed from the beginning

My thanks to Brenda Baker, Vincent Sakowski and Edna
Alford for their helpful comments on earlier versions of
the manuscript; to the Saskatchewan Arts Board and
the Canada Council for financial support; to Wendy Lamb
for her insight; and to Lucy, Darwin and Rush
for their inspiration.

MY FATHER

My father, Percival Montmount, died in the Congo after lunch on a Sunday three years ago. I was fourteen. He was an anthropologist, then living with a tribe of blue-skinned pygmies who gathered fruits from the fronds of midget trees. We have a picture of Dad between a pygmy and a plastic-looking tree. Dad smiles, showing white, perfect teeth. The pygmy looks into the camera, hypnotized.

My dad died the next day. The photo was given to us by a *National Geographic* photographer, a blond hominid named Cindy Mozkowski. She called him a saint, a brilliant ethnographer, and said the pygmies had truly respected Percival of the Shining Forehead.

Ms. Mozkowski wept big tears that slid slowly down her cheeks and landed on our doorstep. Mom wouldn't let her in the house because she had brought bad news. Next it would be bad luck.

Here's how my dad ascended to the department of Heaven reserved for anthropologists. He was lying on his cot one muggy summer day, outlining an essay titled "Why a Pygmy Refers to Himself as We." A tsetse fly stole through the netting and into Dad's tent. It landed on his arm. He brushed it away. It buzzed over to his exposed toe. He wiggled, and the fly shot into the air. Undaunted, it circled around and around and compound-eyeballed Dad's neck. It touched down and bit.

That evening black Azazel sickness conquered my father. The pygmies buried him standing up. He was facing the sunrise so that he could be carried off to the next world. It was their custom.

It's what Dad wanted. It was in his will.

second prologue

MY FATHER'S EYES

My name is Percival Montmount, Jr., and I have my father's eyes. My eyes are aquamarine like his, set in a thin-boned, eagle-nosed face. But the similarity is more than a physical trait: I have my father's *eyes*. The night he died, Dad materialized at my bedside, extended a ghost arm, and opened his fingers to reveal a pair of glowing spirit eyes. He gently held the back of my head and inserted the magical orbs into my sockets.

I blinked once . . . darkness. Twice . . . light. Dad waved goodbye as he faded away.

I wept, not knowing whether the tears were mine or my father's.

FIELD JOURNAL

Items to carry on the person:
Reliable pen
Backup pen
Field study notebook
Open mind

one

THE BEGINNING

Let's begin at the beginning. About 3.5 million years ago, a short, hairy hominid called *Australopithecus afarensis* walked on two legs, thus distinguishing himself from his peers. His hobbies were swinging a club and throwing stones, precursors to baseball. His offspring gave birth to taller, less hairy anthropoids, who in their turn birthed more. As the millennia passed, these hominids mutated, shed their body hair, perfected the use of their opposable thumbs and strained the boundaries of their intellect, until at last they built siege engines and sailing ships.

These creatures discovered North America. They engineered primitive cities and formed an unwieldy organization they named government. One particularly keen tribe attempted to walk across the barren Canadian prairies in search of the perfect site for a temperance colony. Confused by the wind's whistling, they wandered north. They camped near a river and named the place after the Cree word for a tasty purple berry: *Missask-quah-toomina*. Saskatoon. This camp grew especially fecund, attracting sufficient hominids to include one motivated biped who convinced the others to build a high school.

Truly, it was the first backward step in 3.5 million years. The second was the invention of football teams.

Justin, a robust member of the Jock Tribe, clutched my collar with meaty digits. His right hand was clenched in a fist.

"Don't!" *Whack.* "Ever!" *Whack.* "Call me!" *Whack. Whack.* "That!" *Whack.* "Again!" *Whack.*

His football ring flashed in and out of my vision, stamping impressions in my cheek that would likely be documented in Grad pictures next Thursday. Justin's features were Cro-Magnon: high forehead, thick skull, broad face. The color of his large gray eyes resembled that of an atomic mushroom cloud. Football season was long over, leaving him with vast reserves of simmering testosterone. I was helping burn them off.

"Got that, you little turd?" He shook me. My limbs flopped, but his grip prevented my collapse. "Don't follow me. Don't even look at me." Justin rapped Stonehenge-sized knuckles on my skull. "Got it?"

I nodded. The signal. Submission. He was Lord of the Apes, the Almighty Banana King. I was a low monkey, not worth his energy. Not worth—

Whack!

An uppercut to the jaw lifted my consciousness from its mortal cage. I floated skyward, watching my body waver back and forth like a pugilist whose brain hasn't processed the message that the last punch knocked him out. I drifted higher. A light opened above me. Was this a harbinger of the fabled afterlife all tribes dream of?

A female voice sang out, "Let him go!" Was it a high priestess come to bring down the temples? The mother goddess herself?

"No problem," Justin grunted, "I'm bored anyway." He shoved my carcass. I suddenly snapped back inside myself, eyes wide with fear. I fell like a cut redwood tree, momentum adding to my body's weight. I neglected to use my hands, so I smacked into the ground and shock waves coursed through my nervous system.

The Busybody Tribe surrounded us, shielding the crude ceremony from Groverly High's windows. Its affiliates goggled. Their eyes were large, their batlike ears stretched high to gather up every vibration and echo. When it became clear that I would do no more than moan, they vacated.

I blinked. Stared at an azure morning sky. Wisps of clouds floated in the air. Birds chirped. It could have been a nature documentary. I was relieved it was Friday.

A face appeared in my line of vision. Female. Blurry. Familiar. I batted my eyelids to clear my watering eyes. It was Elissa, my friend.

"Jesus, Percy! *What happened?*"

Several facial areas felt hot as coals. I rubbed my cranium. "I left my body."

"What?"

"I was floating and this light appeared, coming toward me. Maybe it was the afterlife."

"I think you have a concussion."

I tried to sit up. Not prudent. Pain fused seven lower vertebrae. "I am experiencing severe discomfort."

Elissa leaned over, blocking the morning sun. She was as tall and thin as me, her brown hair bobbed, her elfin face elegantly bisected by a slim nose. Her eyes grew wide and owl-like. They stared now, signaling concern and curiosity. She had epicanthic folds, though no obvious Asian ancestors. A sign that all humans share common traits.

Elissa had engaged in ritual body piercing, not for fashion, but in honor of ancient beliefs. Some African cultures believe that demon spirits fly up a person's nostrils and cause illness. To prevent this, she wore a nose ring. She had also situated one ring at the end of her right eyebrow, an ever-present silver tear flicked to the side.

Her fingertips brushed my cheek. "Ow!" I exclaimed.

"Why'd Justin do it?"

"It was my fault. I strayed into his territory." She helped me sit up; my back cracked with each movement. "He then spoke inciteful words to evoke a response."

"What?" Though Elissa has been my closest friend for years, anthropological vernacular can still escape her. "What did he say?"

"He asked whether you and I engage in sexual intimacy and what I thought of the experience. His exact words were: 'Hey, Percy, what's Freak Girl like in the sack?'"

"Freak Girl," she echoed quietly. "Freak Girl?"

"*His* moniker. Don't let it upset you. The gifted are often shunned by lesser intellects. Darwin himself experienced this throughout his lifetime. Besides, I struck back with a witticism. I likened Justin to a body orifice and he took offense."

"You called him an asshole?"

"Please! I was more specific. I implied he was the

mythical ape rectum that shat across the known universe. You should have seen the look on his face—well, once he figured out it was an insult, that is."

"Oh, Percy." She shook her head. Her earrings, two tiny spiders, swung back and forth.

"I know. Not wise. His machismo dictated he must respond in a physical manner. Obvious, now."

"What got into you? We ignore his type. They aren't our tribe. They don't matter."

Our tribe. Let me explain. Numerous tribes exist in friction at our school. The Logo Tribe exhibits name brands wherever and whenever possible. The Digerati Tribe worships bytes and silicon chips. The Lipstick/Hairspray Tribe performs elaborate appearance alterations to attract mates. The Gee-the-Seventies-Were-Great-Even-Though-I-Wasn't-Born-Yet Tribe has predictable backward habits. The Hockey Tribe subdivides into Oilers, Canadiens, Rangers, and other assorted clans.

And finally there's us, the quasi-omniscient Observers.

We are a cohesive group of two—Elissa and I. We are privileged with a special disposition: We don't like the same music as everyone else, don't wear the same baggy clothes, can't always decode their dialects. We seem to have awakened from a Rip Van Winkle–like sleep to behold the ritualistic world called Grade Twelve. The natives fascinate us.

Justin's thumping was a primitive message: I'd trespassed his territory.

"How do my abrasions look?" I asked.

Elissa smiled. Her braces were removed three months ago, but I am amazed still at the white perfection of her teeth. I'm forever intrigued by mankind's ability to connive improvements on our evolution. "Not too bad," she said. "You'll have bruises for sure."

"He held back. If truly angry he would break at least one bone."

"C'mon, enough sitting around." She helped me to my feet. "We'll be late. You going to tell anyone about him?"

"No point. He reaffirmed he's the alpha male. If I'm careful he won't exhibit again before graduation."

We headed up to Groverly High: a hulking, ancient redbrick edifice centered with long stone steps leading to gigantic oak doors. Ascending the steps, you are forced to look directly up at the face of the school. Glorify the architect. See the vision of forefather Walter Groverly, who blessed the architect's design. See there is no escape—the moatlike river blocks off the rear, the street outlines the front. The building has a hundred windows, yet none at ground level. Escape impossible. A perfect plan.

Until Willard Spokes, that is. One year ago, he fell in love with Marcia Grady of the Lipstick/Hairspray Tribe. Willard was too shy to express his amorous feelings. Upon discovering that Marcia dated a basketball player, Willard picked the lock of the belfry and jumped from the tower. He smashed on the cement four stories below. This was after the morning bell rang, so only stragglers witnessed the event.

Willard didn't regain consciousness. After three days in the ICU, he passed to the next world while his mother held his hand. If not for that aerial misadventure, he'd have graduated this coming Thursday too.

He'd be grinning like a plump simian and cracking jokes. He was a leading member of the Smile Tribe.

Onward. When you step through Groverly's gigantic oak doors, you enter an über-hallway, standing on hardwood that creaks, suggesting that the building will momentarily collapse under the weight of teenagers and heavy angst.

After my father's untimely departure, money became scarce. My mother was forced to withdraw me from private school and I was sent here for Grade Ten. Groverly still constituted my habitat for six and a half hours a day, five days a week, unless I partook of any G.A.S.A.'s (Groverly After School Activities).

Elissa escorted me to my locker. En route she pointed to a bleached-blond girl. "Madonna Cult—I thought they were extinct." The female was called Karen, and she was the product of a Blue Collar–Lipstick/Hairspray Tribe union. A crucifix and a black pearl necklace hung between her net shirt–girded mammae.

"Definitely," I agreed. "Sad, isn't it? Clinging to the past. Not even Madonna's dance tracks could revive her cult. A tribe in decline—uh-oh." I bent down so my head wasn't visible through the masses, a reflex bequeathed by my hominid ancestors, who would crouch in marsh reeds to avoid predators.

Elissa also scrunched down. "Uh-oh what?"

I glanced over my shoulder. "Michael and Nicole sighting."

She giggled. "The Jesus Freaks."

"The Born-Again Tribe," I corrected. "I don't want their antievolution chant again. It's always so . . . circular."

Elissa stood and stretched her neck, ostrichlike.

"They're gone. Heading for homeroom. Punctual as Jesus commanded, I guess." She glanced at her portable chronometer, a Gucci. "Two minutes to the ritual sounding of the bell. You ready for algebra?"

I straightened my back. Major pain sparked from seven vertebrae. "Y-yes."

"Ah, the study of the incestuous breeding of numbers and letters. Invented by Professor Algebrady. Objective: to induce coma."

I smiled. Elissa invented fake histories for all our classes. She produced her reliable pen and printed the words *believe nothing* across her binder. She replaced the writing utensil in her shirt pocket and held up the notebook. "Today's motto! Did you know handwriting is a 'makework' invention? A monk liked its appearance, so he made his novices use it. Then civilizations worldwide mimicked the style. Printing is faster and clearer. Test it sometime."

"Yeah . . . okay."

Elissa's encyclopedic mind catalogued stacks of anecdotes about our societal fallacies. It was her *raison d'être*. Her parents are trial lawyers, so her house is home to constant allegation, rebuttal and proof. And expensive furniture no one sits on.

"So you're okay?" she asked.

"Yes. Just a hazard of my job."

"Maybe splash water on your face. At least clean the scratches; you know how bacteria love open wounds. Could contract the flesh-eating disease and expire before second period."

I smiled. The bell clanged like a fire alarm.

I must correct my observation. There was no bell,

only an electronic recording of one. It had the same effect, though.

"Assimilation time," I announced. We assumed our impartial anthro faces. Elissa amalgamated with the crowd, her head bobbing.

I headed into the field. Four steps later a deep voice commanded, "Percy Montmount, come here."

It was the leader of all the Groverly High strata. He-Whose-First-Name-Is-Too-Sacred-to-Speak.

Principal Michaels.

two

THE LUCK OF THE BEOTHUKS

Michaels waved me toward his office. He was adept at using his gargantuan hands to communicate. I obeyed. Justin sat in the outer waiting room, conducting a staredown with the floor—a sitzkrieg. He took time out to glower at me. I exhibited no antagonistic behaviors.

I hesitated at the door to the inner sanctum. What was protocol? Leave it open? Did Principal Michaels wish to display ascendancy to all? Or close the door, thereby inflaming plebeian wonder at the execution of his power?

Principal Michaels sat at his desk. His hand signaled *Close the door.*

I did so. He gestured to an adjacent wooden chair. I sat. His use of nonverbal signals was perhaps intended to intimidate me.

The office was spacious and clean, every book shelved, binding face out, and every spit-polished wall plaque hung squarely. The desk was exactly in the center of the room.

"Hello, Percy," he said carefully. "How. Are. You.

Today?" His slow elocution indicated that he assumed I was mentally challenged.

"Fine, I am," I answered, opting to mimic Dr. Seuss.

Principal Michaels cracked a crooked smile. Though a backward hominid, he was amiable. He was ruddy-faced and bald, heavyset, with amazingly thick eyebrows. They replicated two black, well-fed caterpillars clinging midbrow.

"Why are you smirking?" he asked.

"I—I'm sorry. I was preparing to sneeze." And I did. Lightly. Obviously fake.

His blue, serious eyes cooled. "There was a scuffle outside the schoolyard. What are those cuts on your face?"

I held myself rigid. "The result of a biking accident, sir."

"Did you ride your bike this morning?"

I paused. I had walked the three blocks from home. "No. Last night, sir."

"They look fresh. I was told you were in a fight with Justin Anverson."

I had overlooked the fleet-footed tribe of sneaks who lurk, awaiting the chance to insinuate themselves with the school patriarchy, intending to advance their grades and general status.

"First, sir, it was not a fight so much as an insightful interaction. Second, it was my fault. I transgressed the cultural boundaries between tribes, and this provoked him."

The principal's right caterpillar wiggled. "I don't understand. Did you start the fight?"

"It was not a fight. But take comfort: All is aright

now. I know better. I knew all along—I just 'slipped up,' as they say. There will be no future altercations. Guaranteed."

Principal Michaels frowned. The caterpillars clung in place, then inched toward each other. "You're saying there won't be any more fights?"

"I will be mindful of the protocol. I won't trespass again."

Michaels examined me solemnly. "I'll be honest, Percy. I don't know if you're joking or serious. Neither pleases me. Your teachers have told me you've drifted away from your fellow students. And to be frank, some of your behavior is rather odd. Mr. Nicol said he caught you hiding in the dressing room, spying on the boys' soccer team at halftime."

"That incident was misinterpreted. I wasn't spying. I was curious about motivational speeches during athletic competitions. I attempt to be cordial to my peers, sir, but I must not influence their rituals. That's why I was hiding."

"Rituals?"

"Yes." I stopped. How to explain my whole project? "Their rituals," I repeated. "Their lingo, haircuts, special signals, all of that, sir."

His frown remained. "I want you to see Mr. Verplaz. You understand why, don't you?"

The school therapist. Again. He was a singularly valuable hominid. "Of course, sir. I will visit the shaman—I mean Mr. Verplaz."

"I get the feeling you're stressed, Percy. Are you worried about graduation?"

"No. Why?"

"It can be a tough time. Mr. Verplaz will help with coping strategies. I'll also talk to your parents."

I sucked air in sharply.

He had forgotten Dad was dead. Principal Michaels mixed me up with one of the hundreds under his authority, but in that instant I believed he *would* call my father, somehow communicate through the misty nebular spirals of the Netherworld and get a message to Dad.

Tell him . . . Tell him . . .

Tell him I'm trying. I'm trying very, very hard.

"Percy? What's wrong?"

Relief: He paused. I covered my eyes with my hands but quickly pulled them away. Wet palms. Salt stung my cut face. This was not to happen. Another error.

"Is there something . . . ?" Principal Michaels stood and took a hesitant step. "Did I . . . are you . . . all right?"

I stared at my hands. Tears. The universal symptom of emotional distress. "No," I said. "Yes. All right. Everything's all right." I rose, then turned and departed the sanctum.

The bathroom was empty. I must not display emotions to analysands.

I examined my hominid face in the mirror. Long and thin, with bulging chin muscles—a result of nightly tooth-grinding? Beneath short brown hair, a slanted forehead gleaming with a thin sheen. Sweat.

I look sad, lost, concluded the part of my brain that examined. *Poor little* Australo-Percy-ithecus . . . *can't find happiness. Can't control the physical manifestations of grief.*

The voice steeled me. I had made errors in the field. I

needed to concentrate on my task. It was time to perform my ritual. I retreated into a cubicle and closed the door.

I undid the top four buttons on my shirt, exposing a nearly hairless chest. I pushed my hand into my pocket for my container, opened it carefully and extracted a sharpened implement.

There was once a tribe in Newfoundland called the Beothuks. They were skilled canoeists who painted themselves and most everything they owned with red ochre. Don't bother looking for them. They're extinct. They were squeezed to death by Micmacs on one side and fish-hungry Europeans on the other. No longer able to fish their own waters, the shy Beothuks moved inland and starved. The last to be seen by outsiders was Nancy Shanawdithit, who died of TB in 1829. The rest disappeared. Few details of their customs are known.

But I imagined them. Before the final Beothuk died, he had grief to expel, so he traded a bone pendant with the Naskapi for three porcupine quills. He poked his flesh and his sadness leaked out.

I forced the pin through the pale skin around my left nipple. I felt a joyous pain and then . . . release.

I withdrew the pin and repeated the procedure.

I imagined I was the last abandoned, lonely, out-of-luck Beothuk, far away on my island, staring at the sea, longing for my tribe. My people. All gone. Forever. Dead.

I slowly closed the container and with keen deliberation refastened the four buttons.

I took control. I exited the cubicle and left the bathroom.

three

HOME IS A HABITAT

Mom expects the apocalypse daily. She watches for the grand event from Ninth Street, venturing out of our house only when the karma is right and there is no omen that the fabric of the universe will suddenly rip and suck humanity as a vacuum would dust. She admits to hoping doomsday will show the courtesy to wait until after my graduation.

I approached our house at 3:32 P.M., the same time I arrive home every day from school. I, like all humans, am a creature of habit.

I stood in the sun porch, collecting my surging, far-flung thoughts. With the door closed, the outside world was . . . outside. My muscles relaxed. I had survived another day of surveying. A night of cataloging awaited.

Our house hadn't changed since Dad went to the Congo. Its previous owners worshipped at the altar of the Beatles, and had splashed bright orange and red paints on each wall except those in the den, which they painted black. The resourceful decorators then tossed speckled stars into the paint to achieve the semblance of the starlit sky. Mom and Dad loved the house at first sight and changed nothing.

Except: the entranceway. Three years ago Mom installed stained-glass windows in the sun porch. They came from the Cypress Hills. She and Gray Eyes, her shaman, had sneaked out of their sweat lodge, stolen across the prairie grass, and liberated the windows from an abandoned Anglican church that had been converted into a grain bin. The stained glass lends an eerie kaleidoscopic effect to the porch. The light reveals a collection of seven impressionistic phallic paintings on the wall and twelve phallic statues lining the hardwood floor. Interspersed are various clay representations of the naked mother goddess, She-of-the-Mountainous-Bosom.

Even in the old days man was fixated on the size of mammae. We evolve, but some things never change.

I am convinced this exhibit offends the postman. I caught him peering like a priggish pontiff through the mail slot one morning. Mom hopes he peeks more, because the images will rouse his sleeping inner goddess.

She should know. Karmina, my mother, is a psychic. She does life readings (forty-five dollars), palms and tea leaves too (thirty dollars). She comforts worried clients, telling them existence continues after their carbon-based bodies expire. She prospers; everyone frets over the future.

Mother is also a body work specialist for a menagerie of clients. Even the mayor of Saskatoon, who asks for predictions midmassage, partakes of her services. The largest portion of her patrons are New Age *Homo sapiens,* bright-eyed and eternally optimistic. Their spiritual afterimages seem to float around the massage room.

Karmina is my mother's full name. When I was

young, she was Karmen Kristjanna Montmount, but she changed her name after the news about Dad. Karmina is in the yellow pages under *Psychic*—right before a world-famous Texan, Psychic to the Stars. She also appears under *Massage: Karmina, Massage Process, Body Work, Yoga and Colonics.*

"Is that you, Perk?" my mom called from the living room. It's the nickname my father gave me.

"The one and only," I answered, surprised at my peppiness.

"Can we talk?"

"Evolution gave us tongues—we might as well use them."

I pushed through the curtain, the plastic beads kissing and smacking behind me, faintly electrical. Pine and cedar incense fogged the room with forest scent, but a glazed window high in the far wall illuminated the haze. Before me was a jungle of lush green plants hanging from the ceiling.

Mom sat on her white hemp meditation pillow. It was stuffed with old rags because she refused to cushion herself on the plumage of deceased winged vertebrates. She also cringed whenever near a fried chicken restaurant. Her hair was unbound; her black-and-gray tresses flowed across her back. Her sallow skin was evidence that she suspected the ozone layer would no longer shield her from the feared ultraviolet.

I assumed the lotus position on a nearby pillow.

"What shall our topic be today?" I asked playfully. "Qi Gong breathing? Stocks and bonds? My report card?"

"Your principal phoned me," she said, her voice soft, calm.

"I expected that." Actually, I had forgotten his promise to call. "I'm sorry he interrupted your day."

"He's worried about you. . . . I'm worried." Silence. Mom stared out of clear blue eyes. "Were you in a fight?" she asked.

I nodded. She watched carefully, decoding my facial movements. A tic indicating unhappiness; a flicker, a lie. Perhaps she was reading the rainbow of colors around my head: my aura.

"Why?" she asked.

This was a multilayered question in Mom's world. She was inquiring: What karmic payments was I charged with? What negative energy compelled a situation that would harm my body? A past-life crime? She believed there were no accidents.

I had to protect her. She lived in a spirit world, easily disturbed.

"I bumped into this guy and he, like, flew off the handle," I said. Mom was more comfortable if I used teen vernacular. "He's, like, always doing this stuff. He's a bully, you know."

"And that was it?"

"He also said something rude about Elissa."

She nodded, digesting this information. "I know you're friends, but that's no reason to get into a fight. There are no good reasons."

Mom had listened to "Give Peace a Chance" far too many times.

"I didn't intend to get involved, Mom. It just happened."

"Things don't just happen. You know that. Did you respond to his rudeness?"

I let out my breath. "I may have said something back. But he deserved it."

"You could have chosen a dignified silence. Remained motionless and nonthreatening. Remember: 'Nonviolence is mightier than the mightiest weapon of destruction.'"

I recognized the quote. "Mom! Gandhi never went to Groverly High. I don't think he was ever a teenager."

"He faced down the British Empire. Your conflict is minor in comparison."

I sighed. How could I argue with that?

"I'm worried, Perk." Her voice was barely audible. "Mr. Michaels said you don't get along with your classmates."

I don't assimilate, was all he meant.

"I have friends, Mom. There's Elissa, and . . ." I strained my memory. A familiar plump face popped into my head. ". . . And Ms. Peters."

"Who?"

"The librarian." She was kind to me—at least she ordered the books I asked for—so she could be considered a friend. "Anyway, that's not the point. Principal Michaels expects me to act like all the homin—the keeners. He wants me to join the establishment." Mom grew up in the sixties, and I had long used words like *establishment* and *Woodstock* to convince her of the rightness of my argument. I stayed away from *free love,* though. A concept she didn't believe applied to teenagers.

She was impassive. "It won't happen again, will it?"

My jungle vibrated with aggressive tribes. Statistically, the chances of a repeat were amazingly high. "No," I said.

If it did happen, I'd ask Justin to only hit me in the gut to hide the bruises.

Mom nodded and closed her eyes, her face serene. I often wondered if she had only one emotion, calm, like an unbroken wave rolling peacefully across the ocean.

"Meditate with me," she said, reaching out. Blindly, unerringly, she found my hands. "Cold palms. Your energy levels are low. Unblock the Qi channels."

I closed my eyes. Her hands were hot. I concentrated on my breath, slowing it down, imagining energy coming in through my belly button, up my torso, across my shoulders and down my arms. I'd been doing this special breathing combined with yoga and Tai Chi since I was a child. After a few minutes my hands warmed.

I found my center. Calm. Still. Not bliss, but close enough. After a time, I slowly withdrew my hands.

A motorcycle passed the house, muffler growling. Groggy, I looked toward the sound. The trance was broken. I rubbed my burning palms together, massaged my temples.

Karmina "Gandhi" was at peace. She really did have amazing control over her body and emotions.

She suddenly lifted her head. Her eyelids snapped open. "I contacted your father about all this and reminded him that graduation is coming up. I don't know if he'll appear or not."

Typical Mom. She "spoke" to Dad regularly. With a Ouija board? Perhaps a three-way Ouija call, with Principal Michaels in there too.

Hello, Percival Montmount senior? Sorry to disturb your afterlife; it's about your son.

A pain grew in my chest, right next to my heart. My nipples ached. "I have to go to my room, okay?"

Mom examined me with all-seeing eyes. Several moments passed. "Yes, okay," she answered, "it's all okay."

four

PROM HOMINID

Corvus the crow stared as I entered my room. His eyes were two marbles. He was perched on top of the TV, his bone-wings spread as though about to fly. He had held that position for two years. Chessy, my skeletal cat, was curled around a clay human skull on my dresser. Scattered across various shelves were Mickus, a mouse; Boris, a bat; several pinned butter-flies; a beetle display (labeled perfectly); a large dragon-fly; a jarred calf fetus; three formaldehyded frogs; and five small blocks of petrified wood. I also possessed several wooden masks and two conical tribal dolls of cloth and beads from South Africa.

Segregated to one side was my collection of plastic *Star Trek* figurines (including my favorite, Dr. McCoy, a.k.a. Bones). They have no anthropological value but deserve a place of honor on my dresser. I spent many hours pretending to be on the U.S.S. *Enterprise* during my youth. I was the ship's anthropologist, a specialist in aliens.

Corvus was my first great taxidermy success. I had discovered his body in the backyard—no apparent cause of death. I brought him into my room and placed him in my aquarium (sans water), along with my dermestid beetle colony (I'd ordered the beetle kit from a company in Montana). These voracious chewers of decaying matter cleaned the flesh from Corvus within a few weeks. I then painstakingly reassembled him, all the time trying to picture his genetic connection to the dinosaurs.

I ran my finger across his furculum, the bone that absorbs the shock of flight. Without it, ol' Corvus would be cracking his hollow bones with every swoosh of his wings (when he was alive, that is). It's also called the wishbone because humans, after consuming a bird, like to take the furculum and pull it apart. Whoever gets the larger piece makes a wish to the heavens. This pagan Etruscan ritual survives to this day—they taught it to the Romans, the Romans brought it to Britain, the Brits brought it here. The past is always with us.

I sat at my desk, surrounded by shelves packed with anthropology books, including several editions of *The Origin of Species,* Darwin's little ditty about natural selection, which set the scientific world buzzing. I had nearly memorized it. Surrounding that were all the latest books on evolution, including one that presented the theory that evolution was the result of aliens fiddling with our DNA. It's a hilarious read.

In the very center of the desk was my field journal, a large scrapbook-sized tome with many hundreds of pages. It bore the title *The Origin of Species Revisited* by Percival Montmount, Jr. In it was every observation I had made about my environment for the past three years.

Normally, I would record the day's events immediately after school, but today I couldn't open it. There was too much to write down. I had to finish digesting the material. Instead, I opened a biography of Darwin.

About an hour later, I went to the kitchen and prepared a large wooden bowl of sprouts, seaweed, black olives, carrot sticks, butter lettuce and feta cheese. We had no specific mealtime. Mom believed you ate when your body informed you it was hungry.

I sat at our table. A second later Mom appeared, chewing on an apple, her reading glasses halfway down her nose. A massive historical novel was clutched in one hand—her only addiction, not counting yogurt-covered almonds.

"You getting enough to eat?" she asked. "There are rice cakes in the cupboard."

"I . . ." I swallowed a rather large chunk of seaweed. "I'm fine. You fruiting it today?"

She dropped the apple core into the compost pail. "Yep. Trying to cleanse myself. Having some intestinal discomfort."

"Oh." Thankfully, she spared me the details. "Hope it goes away."

"It will. You're looking thin. I should get some more beans. And goat's cheese. Would you like that?"

"Sure," I said, straining to sound enthusiastic. What I really wanted was a triple-patty burger. After my day, I needed animal protein. But Mom was haunted by the fearful clucks, bellows and gurgles of the animals she had consumed during her carnivorous years.

Herbivorousness is odd. Plants have the same two

goals as all species: survival and propagation. They can't vocalize, but perhaps they feel pain on a cellular level. When we pull them from the ground we strangle them. And where are the mite activists? Why don't we fret about the daily destruction of the two mite species that live on our faces, shuffling through hair follicles and sebaceous glands, munching dead skin cells? What about the masses of dust mites scuttling across our pillows? Crushed when we lay down our heads.

It's important to remember we are all ecosystems—never truly alone.

"What's on your mind, Perk?" Mom asked. "You're gazing into nothingness again."

I smiled. "I was just thinking that two bugs in the hand are better than one in the bush."

"You lost me."

"Well, I was reading about good ol' Charlie again—"

"Charles Darwin, you mean," she interjected.

"Of course!" I accidentally spat an errant sprout. "He was a bug nut! Totally avid! There was this time in the bush when he had two rare beetles, one in each hand. Every collector's dream. Just then another monster-sized beetle crawled into the open on a piece of bark. Even rarer than the others. 'How do I capture it?' he asked himself. Then the idea hit him. He popped one beetle into his mouth." I mimicked the popping motion. "He reached for the prize beetle. But the beetle in his mouth pooped out an acrid fluid that burned his tongue. He coughed, the beetle leapt to freedom and the other vanished. Funny, hey?"

"Yes, funny. He was just going to stick needles through them anyway, wasn't he?"

"Well, yeah, he was a collector."

Someone knocked. Mom took off her glasses and set them on the table, then answered the door.

Gray Eyes came in. Her shaman. Well, shaman to a number of people, actually. He was lanky and wide-shouldered, a direct descendant of the Vikings. His hair (once blond) was long and gray and thick enough to give a rock star envy. And his eyes really were a mysterious shade of gray. He'd been named by a native elder at a powwow in Banff.

"Hi, Percy," he said. "How's the universe unfolding?"

"The universe doesn't unfold, it expands," I said. "It isn't a sleeping bag. It is expanding at a greater rate every day, but don't be too concerned. That won't affect us for millennia."

Gray Eyes grinned. "You are so magnificently literal, Percy. I wish I could be half as literal as you."

"Thank you," I said. "That's the kindest compliment I've received today."

Mom had slipped her running shoes on. "I'm ready," she announced. She turned to me. "I won't be home until after eleven."

Friday, I thought. Most people would be going to a movie or a bar. But not Mom. "It's sweat lodge night, eh?"

She nodded. "You should go for a walk. Get some fresh air."

"I should," I said, but didn't elaborate. "Have a good time with your pagan ritual."

They both laughed, though I had been serious. I locked the door behind them.

I finished my meal but was still hungry. A mean case of hamburgeritis possessed me. To distract myself, I retired to my room to read *Discovering Archaeology*. The obsession soon subsided.

At 7:45, a finger tapped light as a sparrow on the glass. Elissa stood outside. Long ago she'd stopped using the front door, preferring to enter through my window. The grass below the sill had worn away. I'd placed a chair under the window so she could climb in easily.

I raised the window. In a motion reminiscent of our monkey ancestors, she grasped the bottom of the sill and pulled herself into my room, stepping to the chair, then the floor, and wiping her hands on her pants.

Beautiful. Her entrance, that is. All made possible by eons of evolution: mutations that gave her (and our species) opposable-thumbed hands uniquely qualified to grip the sill.

"What're you staring at?" she asked, with a lopsided smile.

"Nothing." I settled back on the bed.

Elissa plopped on the chair. She wore stylish fatigues and a T-shirt emblazoned with I DON'T KNOW. The shirt had been cut short and revealed a flat abdomen. Her belly button was an innie.

She rested her feet on the bed, saying, "Did you know a guy in Arizona was kicked out of school for wearing a Pepsi shirt on Coke day? Teachers felt he wanted to stir up trouble. Meanwhile students toddle around in shoes made by Third World children enslaved in factories and no one makes a peep. There's no logic to the educational system." She looked across at me, apparently finished. She needed to rant like this once a day. "What you up to?"

"Reading about ancient Egyptians."

"Learn anything new?" she asked.

"Actually it's old. The old worlds. Ancient cultures were able to intuit more about the stars than we know today."

"Did they have weird ceremonies like, say, graduation?"

"No, theirs were advanced societies."

She ran both hands through her hair, making her shirt rise to expose her upper abdomen and lower ribcage. Her mammae were medium-sized. I note this only out of scientific curiosity.

"Have you thought about graduation?" she asked.

"The event itself or the future of the graduates?"

She began playing with a strand of her hair, twirling and untwirling. "The event. All the parties. Not to mention Grad itself. What will it mean? How will it change us?"

"I don't intend to change. It's my—*our*—job to observe the tribal actions."

"Have you thought about the specifics?"

"Like what? The gown? The scroll? The valedictorian address?"

"No, like who you'll take to Grad?"

I blinked. I'd been so wrapped up in anticipating the event, I'd forgotten that society expected me to pick a female partner. Whom would I take? Or, more to the point, who would go with me?

"You. We can study them together."

She grinned. "Are you asking me to Grad?"

"Yes. Isn't that what I said?" She was acting odd. Did she need a signed affidavit?

"Good. Everybody else had a date a month ago. I've turned several guys down while I waited for you."

Other guys had asked her? I tried to picture it but drew a blank. Then: Justin's face. Looming in my mind. No, he couldn't have, their tribes were so different.

Elissa crawled onto the bed and curled across the end. She had never reclined there before. But here she was, transgressing my territory, head propped on hand. Staring warmly.

She was acting . . . well, like she was attracted to me.

That couldn't be. And yet . . . My breath quickened.

This was one part of the human equation I knew little about. Well, nothing, actually. I'd never been on a date. I wondered what it would be like to hold her. She had inviting lips.

But we were professionals. Partners. Friends. It wouldn't be right.

Elissa touched my knee and I jerked. "Have you recovered from battling Goliath?"

"I wear the bruises proudly. Wounds from the field."

She gave me a flicker of a smile. Her large eyes were soft with emotion. Watching me. I was momentarily amazed by them; how did our cells decide to form eyes? What was it like when the first amphibian orbs opened to the world?

"I've been thinking about you a lot," she said.

"Oh?" Everyone was thinking of me today. Principal Michaels, Mom, Justin.

"Yeah, it's not like you to piss someone off. Even a reptile like Justin. You've been so uptight this last month."

Uptight? Emotional turmoil wasn't in my code.

"What set you off?" she asked.

I shook my head. "It was an unexpurgated outburst. It won't be repeated."

"Talk to me in your real voice, Percy."

Real voice? I only had one voice. "Pardon me?"

"Why did you get into that fight?"

I was tired of the same question. This was Elissa's second time in eleven hours. Her eyes wouldn't leave me. "I allowed myself to become involved in the situation," I slowly explained. "That's not good protocol."

"Why did you get into the fight?" Her smile was gone, her face tight, eyes squinting as if at a blinding light.

"It was an accident, Elissa. A miscalculation. I don't want to examine it anymore."

She nodded slowly. "I just wondered if it had to do with Willard."

I bit the inside of my cheek. "Willard," I said.

"Today's the anniversary of his death."

Why would she think I was connected to Willard? A bizarre leap of logic about the student who leapt off our school belfry. "I haven't even thought of him," I lied. I *had* thought of him as we walked toward the school this morning. "Why would this be about Willard?"

"He *was* your best friend, Percy. And mine. I can't stop thinking about him. And I don't know if anyone notices that he's gone."

Best friend? Yes, I had spent time with Willard. We had gone to movies. Exchanged books. Played video games (at his place). An image flashed in my mind: Willard standing outside my window in a downpour, smiling, looking like a drowned rodent. The memory Mesozoic old. He'd taught Elissa the habit of climbing in my window.

I *had* visited him in the hospital; that's how I knew his mother was holding his hand when he died. I'd sat in a chair in the corner waiting for him to wake. If I was there, then I was his friend. Maybe even his best friend.

Elissa cleared her throat. I couldn't find any words. Finally, I opened my mouth. "I overheard a teacher talking about lowering the flag to half-mast."

"Who?"

"Principal Michaels," I lied. Lying is immoral in our culture, but this "news" seemed to cheer her up.

"At least they're thinking of him," she said.

"Yes, they are."

We were silent for a very long time. Elissa repeatedly traced a pattern in my bedcover. Her circling finger entranced me.

"I'm happy we're going to Grad together," she said without looking up. I didn't answer. Her finger stopped.

"I, too, am pleased," I admitted. And I was: How many teens had spent angst-filled hours struggling to procure a prom date? I had avoided that pain.

I'd wear a suit, of course. To fit in. And Elissa would be in a long dress. Maybe something with a low-cut back. She had a beautiful spine. This also I note out of scientific curiosity.

"It's all coming to an end." She sounded almost sad. "Four years of Groverly's educational method: bore, bore, repeat, bore. Do you remember that first Halloween?"

"I still have the cavities." We'd dressed up and toured the neighborhood, ringing doorbells, then kneeling so that we looked like kids. No one was fooled, but they gave us loads of candy. Will was there too. We were chased by one brute who thought we'd egged his window. We hid by the river, snickering quietly, bonding and devouring caramels. "I can't believe we dressed like clowns."

"Clowns?" Elissa said. "We were aliens. Geez, nice memory you have."

I blinked. Aliens. Yet I clearly remembered clowns. One of us was wrong. But I wouldn't argue forcefully. The hippocampus is a notoriously poor recorder of memories. I wouldn't trust it as far as I could throw it.

"If you'd stayed in that private school you'd be ultra-stuffy by now," Elissa said. "Will and I really loosened you up."

"Gee, yeah," I answered. Stuffy? "I didn't want to leave St. Joseph's. But it ended up being a perfect new beginning. A rebirth. I wouldn't trade the experience for anything."

"Funny how things work out," she said.

We mused separately for a few moments. Then a familiar desire came over me. An *intellectual* desire.

"May I see your foot?" I asked.

Elissa looked up sharply as if I'd poked her with a pin. Then she rolled her eyes. "Not again."

"It is scientific curiosity, nothing else," I intoned. She didn't move. "Please," I added.

"You sure you don't have a fetish?"

"I'm certain."

She sat up and rolled down her right black sock, slowly displaying a typical human foot, complete with five toes, ascending in size. Her nails were painted a rainbow of colors. She swung her foot closer. There was nothing out of the ordinary.

"Please spread your toes."

"Whatever you command, kinky boy." She giggled.

I ignored her and waited patiently, though I admit my heart palpitated and my breathing became shallow. Slowly Elissa spread her toes. Thin webs of skin opened between them, joining her digits like a frog's. I sighed. Here it was. A webbed foot. A genetic leftover from our days as ocean-bound vertebrates. Or perhaps it was a recent mutation, the water beckoning us back home. After all, as embryos we humans do have gill pouches. One small step from becoming amphibians.

"That is the most spectacular foot I have ever seen," I whispered. Oddly enough, her other one was normal.

She wiggled her toes. "Try shoving it into sandals."

"Are you certain you don't swim any faster?"

"Not that I've noticed."

"Do you ever feel an urge to dive in the ocean?"

"What? Not really." She folded her arms. "My toes are tired of being on show."

"Thank you," I said, and I meant it. I owed her for showing me this wonder, and I thanked whatever lines of consequence had supplied a friend with a webbed foot.

"You're the weirdest person I've ever met, Percy junior." She laughed as she pulled on her sock, her eyes bright. "Weirdest to the utmost."

* * *

Later that night I opened my field journal.

I sketched the evolution of fins to feet and back again.

Then wrote an article titled *Codes of Violence: The Jock Tribe.*

When my hand cramped two and one third hours later I put down the pen. I went to bed and my thoughts turned to our greatest ancestor: *Australopithecus afarensis Lucy.* She was 3.2 million years old, the closest hominid to the missing link. Lucy and her relatives were likely the first to walk upright.

I wondered if Lucy's toes had been like Elissa's.

five

CARNIVORE

Like a gastronomical boomerang, my desire for a hamburger returned and shadowed me all Saturday morning. By early afternoon I found myself on Broadway, strolling past the restaurants and cafés, salivating. Most, except the Taj Mahal, were *verboten* to Mom.

But she had gone to Wanuskewin for a nature walk and would be spending the night with friends in the traditional teepees that were part of the park (this accommodation was $79 per person, hallucinatory dreams not included). This meant I was free to indulge. She'd never once told me not to consume meat, but anytime I had she'd smelled it on me or heard the ghostly moo of the cow. Then she'd give me a look of absolute disappointment.

But today I had to explore my inner carnivore. I slipped into the Broadway Café and ordered a triple burger with fries and gravy. It arrived steaming hot, on a platter-sized plate. I quickly devoured my meal.

Then: tears. Almost. I blinked them back. This used to be my time with Dad. We'd sneak away from Mom and what he called the "infernal sprouts" and come here to gorge ourselves. He'd tell me about all the odd things he'd eaten while in the field (goats' eyeballs being his favorite). Then he'd slip me a stick of peppermint gum and say, "She'll never know." We'd slink back, keeping our distance from the matriarch.

I had swallowed a five-pound weight. My digestive system, trained on sprouts and celery, was at a loss. The hamburger seemed to be gaining mass by the second. The best action: walk it off.

I paid my bill, bought gum (peppermint) and proceeded toward the river, chewing. Soon I was strolling along the Meewasin Trail, staring across the river. This was a time to surrender the minutiae of my life and concentrate on the bigger picture. Where was evolution taking humanity?

I pictured Elissa's foot. Then her ankle. Her midriff. I shook my head. This wasn't the direction I'd intended.

I tried something different: the double helix. Encoded in our genes was almost every step of our evolution. Scientists had mapped the gene; now I had to find a way to follow that map to the beginning. Maybe there was information on the Internet that would help me.

The hair on the back of my neck suddenly tingled. A keen anthropologist develops a sixth sense. I looked up. A familiar broad-shouldered male lumbered around a corner.

I quickly inserted myself into nearby bushes, folded the greenery around me and crouched down. My heart thudded and a sheen of sweat coated my forehead. This attracted the attention of a fly, which tasted my perspiration with its feet. I tried not to think of the fly's previous explorations. A second fly descended. A third. I blinked, raised my eyebrows.

I willed: stillness. In the jungle I would have to deal with hordes of insects. I, Percy Montmount, Jr., could persevere.

Then: Thick trunklike legs became visible through the foliage. I looked up, moving only my eyeballs. Justin loomed. Could he scent me out?

"How're you doing, buddy?" he asked.

I made no response.

"Would you like some ice cream?"

Was this an attempt to bribe me out of my cover?

"You're pretty quiet today."

I held my breath. The legs moved down the paved path.

When I was sure Justin was a good distance away, I slipped into the open, nearly bumping into an ancient woman with a walker, a matriarch of the Denture Tribe. "You playing hide-and-seek, son?" she asked.

I shook my head.

Justin was slouching under the bridge, a little boy riding his massive shoulders. My eyes widened. I blinked, watched them disappear.

I followed, my right hand automatically reaching into my pants pocket, retrieving my field notebook. I wrote as I walked. Could this be a breakthrough? Justin displaying affection/protection in public. Was this a brother—a young Justin in the making? To be trained in the ways of the Jock Tribe? At what point did the rituals begin?

They stopped at a park bench and I stole under the bridge, using the shadows for cover.

Justin lowered his brother onto a bench, then sat beside him. They appeared to be talking. Justin tickled the young recruit. The boy giggle-shrieked. Justin wrapped him up in his arms.

I was stunned. I stepped into the open. Justin looked up, still hugging. His eyes narrowed.

I retreated, keeping the pillars between me and them. Then I scrambled up the hill on the other side of the bridge and headed for home, clutching my field notebook like a shield.

six

NAKED AND TIED TO A STICK

My father was always leaving. Most of my paternal memories are snapshots of him loading suitcases into the trunk of a taxi, a sun hat shielding his bald head. Or he'd be standing in line at the airport, backpack slung over one shoulder, flight tickets in hand. He'd perform a wiggly-fingered wave, then disappear through the departure gate. Mom would lead me to the window and we'd wave to his plane. Well, we'd wave to all the planes to be sure we got the right one. Whenever I see a jet bisecting the sky I think of Dad.

His destinations were glorious: the Australian outback, the Far East, Peru, the thick urban jungles of Hong Kong. Places where wondrous events occurred daily. Where dreams came to life. Sometimes we'd read about Dad in the back pages of one of the national papers, see a grainy photo of him standing beside an ancient statue or sitting among African tribesmen.

Invariably, two months, three months, even six months later, Dad would return and wrap me up in his arms, smelling of sweat and strange smoke. He'd give me a whisker rub. He'd kiss Mom. And we'd take him home. Glorious Dad, back in our little house.

That night, and many nights after, I would wait in my bed, vibrating with excitement. Story time. He'd open his mouth and spin tales long into the night.

My favorite was about how he'd outsmarted the RanRans, a cannibal tribe in the Roterwali Peninsula, near the Amazon River.

Dad was studying the peaceful Wanniwa. During the night the RanRans stormed the village, drove the men away and stole whichever women they could capture. When Dad poked his head out of his hut to check on the commotion, the invaders stopped and gawked at the first white man they had ever seen. He was in a typical anthro outfit: khaki shorts and shirt, un-kempt hair (what there was of it) and a pen and pad of paper in hand.

The RanRans encircled him with bamboo spears, poked and prodded him through the jungle vines to their canoes, then paddled vigorously down an Ama-zonian tributary teeming with piranha. They stared the whole time. Even warriors in the other boats steered close to eyeball Dad.

At daybreak they arrived at their village. A wall of bamboo spikes crowned with impaled shrunken heads surrounded their homes, dome-shaped huts jutting from the earth. The cries of birds and wild monkeys filled the air.

There's a Bugs Bunny cartoon in which cannibals boil a large pot of water, slicing onions and carrots into it. Then they attempt to force Bugs in, managing only to steam his tail. This potboiling motif is a common misrepresentation. Cannibals tend to bash your head and slice and dice you on the spot. Then they boil you. It's similar to our treatment of cattle.

My father was fortunate because this tribe had strict traditions for food preparation: First the meat was sweated to cleanse it of evil spirits. So, they stripped Dad and tied him to a stake for three days, allowing him only a bowl of water and a handful of fat grubs. He ate the grubs happily because he recognized the nutritional value inside their slimy bodies. Still, he disliked how they wiggled down his throat and quivered in his stomach before succumbing to gastric acid.

The RanRans quizzed him nonstop. Where were you born? Did you come from a white-shelled egg? Were you birthed under a full moon so that the light whitened you?

My father remained silent, stoic. He knew enough of the RanRan language that he could have begged for freedom, but he chose to quietly endure the three-day torture, which left his balding head scorched and his eyes red and dry. Army ants crawled over his entire body, biting him. The tribe believed the ants would tenderize the meat and release the tiny demons trapped by the skin. Dad watched the sun and the stars, kept track of the days, so that even though he was naked and without a watch, he could have told you the time.

They finally untied him and marched him to the roasting pit. He was bound to a spit over a mound of kindling. The RanRans' custom was to cook their food alive because screaming would loosen the flesh from the bones. They began to make fire, spinning a piece of wood inside a wooden groove to create friction. Just as the smoke appeared, Dad said, *"Kewokee nok nig,"* which meant "Something bad will happen."

The RanRans were shocked. The chieftain said, *"Blegin blog,"* which translated to "Of course." They assumed Dad meant something bad would happen to him. They laughed uproariously, patting each other on the back and slapping their own cheeks, which was their jovial habit.

He repeated his warning and they guffawed and cheek-slapped again. Finally the chieftain approached with a flame. Dad uttered a third warning and the sky grew dark. The chief pulled back the torch and gawked up.

Above them, the sun was going out.

It was a total eclipse. Darkness rushed over the camp. Flocks of birds fled, confused by the sudden withdrawal of light. Only the corona of the sun was visible, burning like the eye of an angry fire god.

The chief RanRan dropped the torch and fled, followed by his tribesmen. The torch sputtered and died.

Within a few minutes Dad had wriggled out of his bonds and the eclipse had ended. The village was deserted.

"Remember, Perk," Dad would always say, announcing the end of the story, "even when you're naked and tied to a stick, there will always be a way out."

It's my motto.

seven

TRAPDOOR

Elissa had chosen a tiny skull and crossbones as her eyebrow ring. "It symbolizes the end," she explained, "the death of our high school personas. This is the final week before we become free."

"Clever," I said. We were in our usual position next to my locker. A cornucopia of humanity had disgorged before us, oddly active for a Monday morning. "They all look so invigorated."

"It's like a drug. Adrenaline rises as Grad approaches. They rush toward oblivion. So are you ready for the parties?"

"Ready?" I echoed. "I'm psychologically pumped. Test me. I dare you."

She laughed. "Okay, Darwin." She knew I loved it when she compared me to my hero. "Let's start with Tacky Party."

"A cross-tribal function. Dress: multicolored clothes. Drink: Yuk-a-flux, a concoction of alcohol and fruit juice. Music: loud. Time: tonight."

She whistled appreciation. A junior looked our way

and she winked at him. He blushed. I was momentarily jealous.

"Round two," she announced, "the High Tea."

"Easy! Time: tomorrow afternoon. Once a female-only ceremony; now both sexes serve their elders tea and edibles. Later it descends into a herbivore-roasting feast: a barbecue."

"Is your mom coming?"

I shook my head. "She couldn't handle the smell of burning meat. Plus she teaches yoga then."

"My parents can't make it either. Too busy. Guess we'll be each other's parents. The rest of the week's going to be a blast."

"Yes, the River Party, Neolithic to the extreme. And, finally, ritual of all rituals, the All-Night Grad Party."

"It's a casino this year."

"Ha!" I exclaimed. "We can bet on the odds of Justin evolving."

"Or making it through first-year university," Elissa quipped.

We smiled at each other and she touched my cheek. "Hardly a bruise. You've healed well." Her fingers were warm. *Healing hands,* I thought. *She has healing hands.* The bell rang.

"Take care of yourself," she said, lowering her hand.

"I will," I answered. "I—I'm happy you're going to Grad with me."

She blushed. "Me too, my anthropological angel. Me too."

I was overcome with the urge to hug her. I reached out, felt suddenly awkward and decided to pat her back. "Grad's gonna rock, I promise." We headed our separate ways.

Time passed with ease. Our teachers smiled, dispensing the last bits of their curriculum into our 1,350-cubic-centimeter brains. Some great witch doctor had greased the wheels of education, and they spun madly.

They stopped spinning at two o'clock, when I raised my hand in English 30. Ms. Nystrom, a kind teacher with a large birthmark on her left cheek, cocked her head and frowned. "Percy, you have something to say about Shakespeare?"

"Yes, I do." I stood up. The faces of my fellow students expressed a mild curiosity, as though a large insect had rested on my forehead. "Shakespeare was an amazing *Homo sapiens,* but his volumes of creative output can be reduced to one impulse: survival. His plays shouldn't be valued as works of art but as scientific proof of how complicated survival instincts have become. His creations were a means to secure food and shelter."

I continued. I cannot remember all I said, though I did trace the history of man's evolution from an anthropoid ancestor to clarify my point. The bell rang. The class immediately shuffled out. I paused in mid-oration. Enlightenment was not their goal. I glanced at Ms. Nystrom, but she was memorizing a spot on her desk.

I hadn't meant to go on at such length. It had just happened. I gathered my books and stumbled into the hall.

Where I ran into the past.

Delmar Brass stood there like a tree, an algebra book clutched in his hand. He was a tall First Nations

Saulteaux whose great-great-grandmother had been a member of Sitting Bull's tribe. They had fled to Canada after defeating an American army led by General George Armstrong Custer. They settled briefly in southern Saskatchewan. Most returned to their homeland, though Delmar's relatives chose to stay. I had once interviewed him for an article detailing the influence of cowboy movies on modern perceptions of natives. *Anthropology Today* never published it. In fact, no major scientific magazine expressed interest. My groundbreaking theories intimidated them.

Every time I saw Delmar I thought of the bison running over the plains, the grass growing tall and wild, no European-style cities darkening the land.

"Hear you were in a fight," Delmar said. "Need help?"

His eyes were dark, his hair black and tied back. He had developed an affection for me after the interview—that is, he occasionally nodded in my direction. Even once when he was with his friends.

"The situation is resolved. Thank you."

"Good. Take care." He continued down the hall, his tread surprisingly light.

I deposited my books, examined my watch: 2:35. Time for my appointment with Mr. Verplaz, the school shaman, He-Who-Lives-on-the-Top-Floor. A last-ditch attempt to correct the wayward.

At the very least, it would be a stimulating conversation. Plus he kept a jar of lollipops. I'd get a treat.

I walked slowly, deliberately. On the second flight of stairs, I became aware of the motion of my feet, pictured our ancient ancestors taking their first wobbly steps.

"Why you staring at your feet, Montmount? Afraid you're gonna trip?"

Justin loomed on the landing above me. Had he marked it and the soft-drink machine with his urine? Had I trespassed his territory?

"I was trying to figure out why we walk upright."

He shook his head. "You're retarded, aren't you? How's your face?"

His tone conveyed no concern, but I replied as if it had: "A scratch and a slight bruise. Thank you for the lesson in tribal interaction."

He glared. "What was that crap in English? Our last class and you barf up another lecture. I should give you a smack." He clenched his ham-sized fist, looked at it; then his eyes flicked back to me. "You followed me in the park, didn't you?"

"I was only there to clear my thoughts."

"Spying is more like it. Again."

"I don't spy. I observe."

"Whatever." He spat. The spittle landed near my feet. "We're sick of you."

"We?" Was he having a dual-personality problem?

"Everyone at school. *All* the students. You stare like we're freaks. But you're the freak."

I blinked. "I am not a freak. I'm not. I'm just trying to do my job. I didn't intend to disrupt your behavior."

A strange reaction followed: He looked genuinely sad. "You don't even speak English, do you? Just that quasi-science crap."

"I do speak English. It's the language of my culture."

He furrowed his brow, a look I imagined the Cro-Magnons got when they first saw something beyond their ken. "You and your weirdo friend are first-class losers."

I narrowed my eyes and clenched turnip-sized hands. "Did you ask Elissa to Grad, you . . . you big ape?" My heart pounded madly. I was shocked at my reaction and disappointed at the blandness of my insult. "No, wait . . ." I jabbed a finger in his direction. "Classifying you as an ape would be an insult to apes and all other simians." I sucked in a deep breath. "Did you ask her?"

Justin's brow furrowed even deeper. "Ask Freak Girl to Grad? I'm not desperate."

I glowered, silently.

He pointed. "Four days, Ugly, and we're done. Just be careful, Einstein." He turned and lumbered down the steps.

What interesting behavior, I thought. *What very, very interesting behavior.* I *was* slightly insulted. Calling me Einstein. *Hmmph.* Einstein was good, but he was no Darwin.

I walked up the next flight, letting my clenched hands relax.

The rooms on the top floor of Groverly High were mostly vacant. The fluorescent lights glowed dully; two of the bulbs were burned out and a third flickered madly.

A large abandoned art studio ran along one side. I plodded down the hall, passing under a trapdoor with an oversized padlock. This was probably where Willard had climbed to the roof.

"Percival," a voice whispered from the other side of

the trapdoor. I looked up, straining my sensory system. Something skittered across the wooden panels. My throat became dry.

Mice, I thought, picturing the beady-eyed rodents. They're always scampering around the school, foraging. It had to be mice.

I backed up. My brain adjusted my synapses so that I became two big ears, listening for another noise. Five steps away I heard a faint *"Percival."*

I turned the corner and leaned on the wall. There was a barred window at the top of the stairs, and I stared at the outside world, somewhat surprised to see daylight. The whisper had to have been my imagination. Or was it an echo of Will's voice? Forever trapped in the belfry.

Shapes moved at the edge of the schoolyard. The Smoker Tribe was gathered like a flock of crows, enjoying spring, their lungs filtering tar and nicotine. I held that position until my biorhythms steadied. I was not beyond superstition; the voice was a sign to avoid Mr. Verplaz.

Then the sound of squeaking hinges. A door?

Or: trapdoor?

I retreated down the stairs.

eight

A WINTER

Monday ended without any fanfare. Elissa and I exited Groverly's front doors. Three days until graduation, then summer holidays, followed by autumn. Which meant one glorious thing: first-year university. A swarming population from across the country and around the world. A hundred times the number of ritual events. My cerebral cortex vibrated with anticipation. I would have to purchase a new journal.

"Put this in your think box," Elissa said as we walked down the stone stairs. "If the highway speed limit were cut in half, most car accident deaths could be avoided. But our society chooses quick delivery of goods over safe travel. Illogical to the extreme! And did you know the majority of car accidents happen near home?"

"I was aware of that."

Her eyebrow ring glinted in the sun. "It's a misleading statistic. People spend more time driving around their neighborhood; it's only natural a greater number of accidents would happen there. Still, we should always be more careful. Especially you."

Was that supposed to be funny? Her words were

hard to follow. What had I been thinking about? Oh, yes, university. Anthropology 110: kindergarten. The professors would see my potential. My promise.

The second coming of Darwin, they would whisper. Just like Montmount senior.

"Something wrong?" she asked.

"No." I walked silently to the edge of the sidewalk.

"Look left before crossing," she warned. Another joke? I stepped off the curb. Car tires shrieked.

Time.

Slowed.

Down.

A car was coming at me. A teen with spiked hair glared through the windshield.

I froze. My survival instincts selected the wrong defense: *Stay still, the predator won't detect movement.* A prehistoric groan of the horn. The knee-high bumper hypnotized me.

I was yanked back and the wheels skidded just centimeters from my body. Air swished past, then another honk. The car didn't stop.

"Look left *and* right," Elissa said, releasing my shirt. "Do you need a crossing guard, Percy? Percy?"

No air. Lungs empty.

"What's wrong, Percy?" Elissa asked, squeezing my shoulder.

"Nothing. Just . . . need to . . . catch my breath." I sucked in. Oxygen! Sweet and pure.

Students on the school steps scowled. The drive-by had been planned. *He's the freak. We're sick of him.* Their common tribal mind spoke in chorus: *Cut him from the gene pool.*

That proved it. Justin was their chief.

I looked both ways, crossed the street. Elissa walked beside me, sneaking glances as if suspecting I might spontaneously combust. A block later Groverly was hidden behind an apartment complex. Students had vanished. I felt safer in this, my own territory.

"Is there something else wrong?" she asked. "You're shaking."

"I ran into Justin again," I admitted.

"What happened?"

"He said everyone hated me," I reported.

"That ugly Neanderthal!" Her vehemence was surprising.

"He's a Cro-Magnon. Neandertal is too evolved," I said. "The Neandertals had a larger cranium and perhaps weren't related to us. Justin has many human tendencies. Bad ones." I resisted correcting Elissa's pronunciation: she had said Neander*thal,* but the proper spelling is *Neandertal.* The word comes from the German and they now drop the silent *h.* "Please don't get upset. Cro-Magnon Boy is suffering brain envy. A common Jock Tribe sickness."

Her fists were white-knuckle tight. Her body vibrated. "I could punch him. I'm just so pissed off."

"Elissa, Elissa," I implored, "don't trouble yourself."

She stood still; then her shoulders sagged. "I suppose you're right." She released a deep breath. "Sticks and stones," she said, "just let it go." We carried on, and a few huffs later, she was back to her former mood. "You know, this is nearly the last time we'll walk home together from school. Do you think it'll be like this in university? Percy? Oh, Percy?"

"Yes." Luckily my cerebral cortex had noted her question. "We'll take the bus to university, so we likely won't walk each other home as often."

"How do you do that?"

"Do what?" I asked.

"Shut yourself off."

"I don't understand."

"Never mind. You're distracted. You worried about the party tonight?" We turned the corner to my house.

"The Tacky Party? It will be interesting. I'm not sure what to wear, though."

"Gee, you almost sound excited." She poked me in the ribs. I jerked away in surprise. "Maybe you don't have tacky clothes . . . actually, I take that back."

"What?" I examined my gray pants—two front pockets and a side pocket for field items, pencil and paper. "This is classic urban camouflage."

"You wear grays and blacks, you mean. You're two steps from Goth. Do you have anything with color? We do have to fit in. A T-shirt with flowers? Red pants? Flamingo beach shorts? I've never seen you in shorts."

I pictured the drawers in my dresser, rows of non-colors. She was right. "What will I do?"

She stopped, put one hand on her chest and extended the other as if she'd suddenly become royalty. "Allow *moi* to introduce *moi*-self. Baroness Eleeza Fashionoski. Kiss my proffered hand."

"Excuse me?"

"Kiss it!" she commanded.

I pressed my lips against her digits. Quickly. Caught a scent like strawberry bubble gum.

"You show da proper respect," she said, looking

down her nose. "I permit you to benefit from my fashion advice. We shall embark for my palace with haste."

"Your place?"

"Palace," she corrected. She lifted one eyebrow. "What da baroness vants she gets. Besides"—her accent disappeared—"you *never* walk me all the way home. You're so chronically self-centered." She winked. "It's your duty now. You *are* my prom date."

"I'm an ignoramus!" I admitted. "Let's go to your dwelling."

"Wow. My dwelling." Elissa tousled my hair. "The way you said that almost sounded romantic."

I straightened my locks. My skull tingled where she'd touched it.

We headed down the steep hill to Saskatchewan Crescent, a descent into the realm of the affluent. Houses were bigger here, sprouting from expansive lots alongside three-car garages, gazebos and crescent-shaped brick driveways.

"Columns are so passé," Elissa said, motioning toward a row of the architectural wonders on one house. "You'd think we were in Rome. *Invita Minerva,* baby!" She yelled.

Elissa also had an interest in an arcane language: Latin. "Which means?" I asked.

"Uninspired. Minerva didn't inspire them. She was the goddess of wisdom."

"I knew that," I lied. We turned a corner.

Among Saskatoonians, the closer you lived to water, the higher your status. Her parents had bought riverside property. The front was eighty percent glass: three levels blatantly exposed to the street, displaying their expensive possessions. I thought of Barbie and Ken's house.

Elissa's mom (Heather) and dad (Gregory) were each in their respective offices across the river. As hunters and gatherers of legal documents, they rarely returned to their nest. Elissa often prepared her own meals and once dressed two giant teddy bears in her parents' clothes and seated them at the dinner table. She served an expensive bottle of wine and discussed her allowance. Her parents didn't appreciate the joke or enjoy finding their sole offspring inebriated. Since then her dad has carried the liquor cabinet key on his key ring.

Inside, we were greeted by Fang. He immediately chomped down on my ankles and refused to let go, three kilos of unbridled toy poodle aggression. He was the second line of defense for the household, after the security system. Elissa's father had brought home this bundle of fluff the week after the wine-drinking episode. She swore she wouldn't be bought so easily, but her philosophical stand lasted about ten minutes.

I reached down, patted Fang's head. He rolled over and I scratched his belly. Thousands of years ago one of our ancestors took a wild wolf pup home and tamed it. Soon all the hunter-gatherers wanted one. Now here I was stroking a genetic parody of that wolf.

"Oh, little Fangy hungry!" Elissa exclaimed. Fang wagged his short tail (it had been clipped to impart visual balance to his body). He trotted after her into the kitchen. I trotted after them.

Fang immediately attacked his meal—a baked lamb specialty brand with a supplement that prevented rashes. If forced to live in the wild, Fang would fall apart in a week.

"Little Percy hungry?" Elissa asked. She motioned to a stainless steel fridge. "We have escargot. And peanut butter and jam."

"Do you have any royal jelly?" I asked, grinning.

She didn't get the joke. "What?"

"Royal jelly," I explained, containing my condescension. "When a queen bee dies another is elected by feeding this special jelly to a lucky larva. Royal jelly, get it? As in, I'm royalty."

"Hill-larry-us," she said flatly. "Maybe someday you'll evolve the ability to tell good jokes."

I put my hands on my hips.

"Wait, hold that pose." She lifted a pretend camera. "There! Perfect! *Homo sapiens poutitis,* a sad creature that wishes it had some good comebacks."

"I—I have comebacks. I choose not to lower myself to your level."

"Right," she said. "Now back to reality. Do you know what season you are?"

"What season? Like which is my favorite?"

"No, your season. Skin type, hair type—certain colors that accentuate your looks. Fall, winter, spring, summer. You're a winter, I bet. That means you look better in dark colors." Maybe there was a correlation between season and personality type. This could be the beginning of a groundbreaking thesis. "Don't look so worried. We'll find something completely tacky." Elissa pulled me out of the kitchen, up the stairs and into her room.

She positioned me next to the bed, which was

littered with stuffed mammals, mostly bears. Interesting how we choose the deadliest carnivores to render as playthings. A symbol of our dominance?

"You're actually kind of handsome," Elissa said, *"Homo sapiens Don Juan."*

My cheeks reddened. "Genetics," I mumbled.

She laughed and slid aside a mirrored door. "You look good in darks, so we'll forget about those." She searched, pulling aside sweaters and shirts, pushing back an entire rack of whites and beiges. Her clothes were color-coordinated with amazing precision—the browns went from dark to light brown, the reds and blues followed a similar pattern. She had enough to dress a small !Kung tribe.

Her movements amazed me. Especially her gluteus maximus. What was even more amazing was that she wasn't supposed to be here at all. On earth, that is. She was first formed when her father's semen was placed in a petri dish at a fertility clinic. One of those sixty million sperm united with an egg extracted from Elissa's mother.

You see, evolution had chosen not to continue her parents' genetic line: Her father had lazy sperm—they apparently preferred lounging about watching hockey. Her parents had cheated their biological destiny.

I watched Elissa, extremely happy that she had been able to become a living organism.

"Try these on," she said. A flashy red-and-green blur struck my chest. I closed my arms too late. "Nice catch!"

I looked down at a pair of large, baggy unisex shorts, designed to cover the knees.

"Get me a shirt, too, Miss Fashionoski," I said.

"As you command, Perky." She disappeared into the closet.

I slipped the shorts over my pants. They fit: two flamingo pillowcases on toothpick legs. A large oval mirror hung on the opposite wall. I examined *Australo-Percy-ithecus* in the shorts. I smiled. Elissa was one of the few who could make me feel truly happy.

Elissa. And Willard.

Will.

Willard was smallish and squat. Puberty had been cruel to him, planting an acne minefield under his face. He had a big smile, a high-pitched hyena laugh and a cowlick at the back of his hair that bobbed when he walked.

Once, the three of us went to a *Planet of the Apes* film festival. Grunting like simians, we monkey-walked to a nearby cafe and consumed several banana splits. Giddy with the sugar high, I told them my heart's dream was to be an anthropologist. To search for lost tribes in the jungle. Will said, "That's awesome!"

A year later he told me he loved Marcia Grady. That she was so beautiful he nearly wept when he saw her. It was one of our last conversations.

An ache the size of the La Brea Tar Pits filled me. He had been my friend. We'd shared secrets. Understood each other. And now I hardly remembered him. My brain was haphazardly erasing experiences, changing them.

Elissa emerged from the closet holding two shirts: bright yellow and a rainbow of colors. "Why'd you put the shorts on over your pants?"

"I couldn't very well undress in front of you."

She rolled her eyes. "I had my back turned. You worried I might see your Mickey Mouse briefs?"

"I—I'd never wear that commercialized rodent on my shorts!"

"Touched a nerve, did I?" She looked me over. "They fit, at least. Here, try this." She handed me the rainbow shirt, good camouflage if I had to hide in a parrot cage. "No, take off your T-shirt. Wear this one with a few buttons loose to show off your chest hairs. All two of them."

"I . . . I can't—"

"Don't be so anal. We're tribemates. Like two monkeys. C'mon."

"Yeah, but—"

"Hurry up!"

I undid my shirt, the air-conditioned chill forcing arm hairs to stand on end. She handed me a cotton rainbow; I stuck my arms through the holes. She attempted to button it but nearly choked me. "Too small! Your chest is bigger than I thought. You been working out?" She gave it another try.

"Hey," I said. "I need air."

Elissa let go. "Oops. Sorry. You . . ." She leaned forward, staring at my chest. "Wh-what are those scars?"

I looked down. A ring of white bumps circled my left nipple. My stomach filled with sand. "Ritual scarring. To release the pain."

Cool fingertips explored the marks. "Oh, Percy," she said softly, "oh, Percy."

"They're mine," I whispered. I stepped back and her hand fell away. She wore a look of absolute pity. I closed my eyes. "Mine. Mine."

"It's okay. Everything's so screwed up. Willard's gone. Your dad, too. You're . . . stressed. I understand."

She did? "Everyone. Leaves me. Like the Beothuks," I whispered. "Out of luck. One of them."

Her brow furrowed. "The what?"

I looked at her. Were we really from the same tribe?

I removed the shirt, grabbed my own from the floor and slipped it on. "This clothing, it—it—is not satisfactory," I said.

She still clutched the yellow shirt. "I've got more."

"No. I'll find something at home." I stepped out of the shorts; they fell to the floor. I backed away.

"We can talk, Percy."

"Talk?" Another step back. A third. "I. Must. Go. Home."

"Percy." A whisper. "We're friends. Don't shut me out."

I fled, taking the stairs two at a time, the sun shooting through the giant windows, lighting me up. Lighting the earth. Holding it inexorably in place. As it had for over four billion years.

nine

TRUNK

Within twenty minutes: relief. The skin around my left nipple ached brilliantly. My mind was clear. Copacetic. I cleansed my pin with rubbing alcohol and returned it to the container.

Silence. My mother was teaching a Qi Gong breathing class at the community hall. I sat on the meditation pillow in my room, assumed the lotus position and closed my eyes. Now, to order my thoughts. To analyze my reactions. To—

The phone buzzed. I remained still. The answering machine clicked on. Elissa's voice entered our house via the speaker. "Call me," she said, then coughed and hung up.

I breathed deeply, tightening my stomach muscles— a Tai Chi method I'd learned from Mom. I had a goal: to discover where all of this was leading. Evolution, that is. It pointed forward, indicating an obvious mission for us, a next logical step.

What was it?

I attempted to send my mind back through the millennia, to the source of all life. Somewhere in my brain

65 ⭐

was a link to the first organism with its orders to survive and replicate. Perhaps if I found the beginning, I could ascertain the end.

Green appeared in my mind, with a dark circle in the middle. I was envisioning mitosis—the nucleus dividing to form two nuclei. Chromosomes being copied. Life continuing. This was almost the beginning.

The phone buzzed again—a distant noise. The green faded to black. I concentrated on bringing the image back but failed. I uncrossed my legs, got up and rubbed my aching head. No contact with my primordial ancestors. No answer. Yet.

The light blinked on the answering machine. Automatic response: I pressed the button. *"Call me,"* Elissa's disembodied voice implored. Then: *"Percy, meet you at the party, okay?"*

I replayed the messages several times. I picked up the phone, punched in half her number, then clicked down the receiver. I repeated this procedure, then stood quietly listening to the monotone hum of the line. Soon the phone beeped loudly at me. A sign that I shouldn't call. I returned the phone to its cradle.

I concocted a meal of sprouts and seaweed. While masticating, I pondered Darwin's life. In 1831, at the age of twenty-two, he embarked on H.M.S. *Beagle.* For the next five years he studied animals, bugs, seeds and stones in South America, concentrating on the Galápagos Islands. From his observations he came up with the theory of natural selection. It took him twenty years to complete his first book on the topic.

I didn't have that kind of time. I wanted to understand now. To see the answer. To have that elusive eureka moment.

Time passed. I wandered from room to room, eventually ending up in the basement, where I was surrounded by rows of jarred peaches, pickled beans and bags of rice. The floor was a pad of concrete that supported an octopus furnace with large ducts running every which way across the ceiling. One light hovered in the center of the room like a giant firefly.

I bent under a duct and knelt before an old wooden trunk coated with dust. I opened it. On the top were several yellowed newspapers with headlines like *Local Anthropologist Identifies Mystical Zuni Object, My Life Among the !Kung* and *Montmount Mounts Mount Machu Picchu*. I skimmed the articles, then reached for the prize underneath.

My father's clothes in a neat, perfect pile. First: a canvas hat with a brim that flipped up. As a child I'd often donned the oversized headgear and pranced around the cluttered basement, imagining my father's adventures and shouting out: "Dr. Montmount, I presume!"

I slipped the hat on. It fit perfectly. I dug into the stack, discovering a multicolored shirt and a pair of khaki shorts. I stripped, not feeling the chill, then dressed in my father's outfit. Gently closing the trunk, I ascended the stairs.

I had a party to attend.

ten

THE DELUGE

I committed a fatal error at the Tacky Party.

The festive event was three blocks away at Sandra Woodrick's. I squeezed between several Jock Tribe members who congested the doorway, and helped myself to a pink lemonade–based punch. I sniffed gingerly. Conclusion: alcohol-free. I sipped nonchalantly, bobbing my head to the music. When in Namibia, do as the Namibians do, my father often said. Teens in colored shirts danced wildly through the living room; others sat on couches or the floor shouting to be heard.

I stood near the bathroom, jammed between a bookshelf and a life-sized reproduction of Rodin's *Thinker.* Hung behind him was a framed picture of card-playing canines dressed up like gangsters. I smiled. Anthropomorphism at its best. Mr. and Mrs. Woodrick must have a fabulous sense of humor, judging by the juxtaposition of those two works of art. Or no taste.

My smile faded as Michael and Nicole strode into the room. I ducked, but they veered in my direction like two lions stalking a lone antelope. And here was my fatal error. I broke a basic law of survival: Always have an escape route.

They approached, clad in matching garb: lime-green shorts and bright yellow T-shirts emblazoned with a red sun and a bird bearing a laurel branch. They absolutely *had* to talk to me: God's orders.

You see, they were from the Born-Again Tribe. They viewed me as a misguided mammal and were hell-bent on saving my soul.

"Percy," Michael said, "it's great to see you."

I straightened my back. "It is?"

"Of course." His light blue eyes were ethereal. His face flawless—smooth white skin and a glistening smile. His teeth had been artificially straightened.

"Are you having fun?" Nicole asked. She too had unnaturally perfect teeth; two large, friendly eyes. She tucked a curl of brown hair behind her ear.

"I experience a modicum of enjoyment."

"Modicum!" Michael echoed. "I like that. You have a real gift with words. It's a blessing."

"Thank you." I was flustered. I hadn't expected them to attend this function, had assumed it would be against their beliefs. But here they stood clutching cans of Canada Dry, looking . . .

. . . as if they belonged.

"Fun party!" Michael gushed as he watched the cavorting students. Did he see them as souls, some smudged with the darkness of sin, others shining bright as a thousand candles? "Drink?" He offered a can that dangled from a plastic six-pack holder.

"No, thank you." I raised my glass.

He moved a few centimeters closer. "I have a question for you."

My heart sank. "Not another Wilberforce," I whispered.

"Wilberforce?" Nicole asked.

"Bishop Wilberforce of Oxford," I huffed, annoyed that they didn't know their theological history. "Darwin's archenemy. He gave the *Origin* a bad review. Asked whether man was descended from monkeys on the paternal or maternal side. He knew nothing about science. He died when he fell off his horse and hit his thick head on a stone."

"Oh," Nicole offered. "Really."

Michael's smile hadn't faded. "That's interesting. But what I'm curious about is the fossils. I know you think we're crazy."

"No," I said emphatically, "religious beliefs are not an insanity. All societies consider it normal to believe in supernatural beings and forces."

"So you don't think we're crazy?" Nicole said.

"I just made that point."

"Good to hear." Michael lightly squeezed my shoulder. His hand was warm. I stared down at it until he removed it. "Anyway, about the fossils. You know how they date them and stuff. I asked our study leader why the scientists got it mixed up."

"Mixed up?" I asked. "Oh, that's right. You believe the world is only ten thousand years old."

"You don't have to yell, Percy," Michael said softly, "the music's not that loud. The earth is actually only six thousand years old. Adam was created in 3975 B.C."

Nicole edged closer. "And don't forget that lots of

scientists aren't sure carbon dating even works. Or that evolution is true. It's just another theory."

Michael used his opposable thumb to open the last can of ginger ale. It fizzed, so he brought it to his mouth. "Anyway, it's the fossils we want to talk about. They're real."

"They are?" I asked.

"Yes." Nicole was now face to face with me. They were a spiritual-philosophical tag team. "But you've been fooled by . . . well, you know . . . *him*." She pointed at the floor. "Evolution. Devilution. Soul pollution." It was a tribal chant. "*He* made you think that fossils are millions of years old. He does tell the truth but circles it with lies. You see, Percy, there *were* dinosaurs."

"There were?" I sensed a breakthrough. "In the Bible?"

Michael fielded this question. "On the ark. Two of each species is what God told Noah. And when the ark finally was caught on Mount Ararat, the dinosaurs stepped out into the new world. Rain had swept everything away. There were new diseases. All of the dinosaurs got sick, died, fell into the ocean and were compressed by the weight of the water, hardening their bones instantly into fossils. Do you see?"

"I understand," I answered, though the idea that the ark could hold enough animals to repopulate the world was ludicrous. A population cannot sustain itself with only two of its species: The gene pool would be too small. Not to mention that water pressure can't harden living flesh into stone.

Thankfully, I glimpsed Elissa across the room. She'd

chosen a flashy pink shirt and a giant gardening hat that could have doubled as an umbrella. When she looked at me, I waved. She removed her hat and held it like a shield against her bosom. She was trapped by overexcited dancers.

"You know," I said, turning my attention back to the Born-Again Tribe, "the age of the universe can be measured using the speed of light. Astronomists have devised a formula that proves light from distant stars began traveling toward Earth billions of years ago."

Put that in your philosophical pipe and smoke it, I thought.

"The speed of light has not been measured properly." Nicole spoke carefully, as though to a child. "Everyone knows that."

I slumped.

Michael drained his ginger ale. "You should meet our study leader. He'd like to talk to you. Our Bible study is fun, you know. Not like other churches."

Agitation saturated my nerves. A simple command to get out. *Out.* Elissa was still halfway across the room, surrounded by a chain of revelers doing the locomotion.

"You know, you're okay, Percy," Nicole said, briefly touching my wrist. "You're really okay."

I furrowed my brow. Okay? I was okay? My tear ducts welled up.

"Did I say something wrong?" she asked.

I shook my head. Elissa joined us at last, nodded at Michael and Nicole. They smiled back.

"I . . . I left my stuff in your car," I said to Elissa.

"What stuff?"

"Those . . . uh . . . field notes I took today. I must retrieve them. Now."

"Yes," she said, recognizing the crisis. "Right. You should."

I walked past Michael and Nicole, pulling Elissa along behind me. We wriggled through the sweaty, Yuk-a-flux–soaked congestion. Outside, I sucked in fresh air. Two teens lay gazing skyward. A tribe of skateboarders, heads shaved, some wearing ski hats, rolled again and again over a jump on the sidewalk, like mice endlessly repeating an experiment.

"What was that about?" Elissa asked.

"They—Michael and Nicole—they have all the answers. They're just so . . . happy."

"Yeah, freaky, eh? Sorry I didn't rescue you sooner. But you should have returned my call."

"Oh. I didn't get it." I breathed deeper. "Really, I didn't."

"You're lucky I came. I stopped by your house and your mom had no idea where you were. Why didn't you call me?"

"I—I just couldn't . . ."

Her look softened. "Are you upset that I saw your scars?"

"No, I'm not. I'm not."

"Don't . . . don't get worked up." She grabbed my hand, squeezed it gently between both of hers as if she'd caught a butterfly. "You take everything so seriously."

I had to take things seriously. How else would I get

my work done? "Elissa, I . . ." My thoughts were too random to express. "I'm sorry. I—I hurt. You. Your feelings, I mean. I didn't intend. To."

"Percy, it's . . . I think I understand. Well, not everything: Who in Hades were the Beothuks?" She grinned.

I laughed. I couldn't help it. "A tribe. In Newfoundland. They painted themselves with red ochre. They died out."

"I see," she said. "Now I do know everything." She squeezed my hands. "This'll all blow over soon. We'll spend the summer catching rays and drinking daiquiris. We'll survive Grad Week. Where there's a will there's a way."

It was one of Will's favorite sayings. A joke. I pulled back my hand. "I could have stopped him," I said. "Should have."

"Will, you mean?"

"He told me. About Marcia. He asked whether I thought he stood a chance with her. I—I was too forthright: I said it was unlikely. She wasn't from our tribe."

"You couldn't have done anything, Percy. Sometimes things just happen."

"Things never just happen," I said. "There's always a reason. I wish I'd lied."

"That wouldn't have changed a thing. It was more than just Marcia. He was—he just kept so much to himself. Who knows what he was thinking half the time?"

"Did he tell you about his crush on her?" I asked.

"Yes. I almost fell over backward to hear him talk about his own feelings. And not joke about them."

"What did you say when he told you?"

"I—I don't really remember. Something like it was good to fall in love. Something like that."

She'd been encouraging. Loving, not logical. "He was lucky to have you as a friend."

"He was lucky to have both of us," she said. "And we were lucky to know him."

I opened my mouth to say something else, but Elissa put a finger to my open lips. "Shhh," she whispered. "You're getting that dazed look. It always happens when you think too much." Her skin tasted salty. She pulled her finger away, put it to her lips. "Shhh. Just forget about everything for now."

I nodded. She grabbed my hand and led me onto the street. "Enough tribal interactions for tonight," she said. "One can only be tacky for so long."

We wandered along silently for several blocks. She didn't let go of my hand. I tried not to think about what this might mean, concentrated on enjoying the warmth of her skin. We walked onto Broadway, into the bright neon lights of the bars and restaurants. Cutting across the street, we took a dark lane instead.

"By the way," Elissa said finally, "I like your hat. It's very cool."

Pride swelled up, but then Dad's hat felt loose, as if a small wind might lift it from my head. Without thinking, I pulled my hand from hers and held the hat down. After several steps I realized my mistake.

Stupid. Stupid me.

Though we walked together for another twenty minutes, I never found the guts to reclaim her hand.

*   *   *

At midnight, Elissa and I hugged in front of my house. For a long time. Then I went inside, my legs all wobbly.

Mom was meditating in the living room, surrounded by candles and a haze of pine incense. *Ommmmmmm* emanated from somewhere deep inside her throat. Her lips didn't move. She could *Ommm* for hours, contacting various internal organs, willing them to function in perfect harmony with the rest of her body and the universe.

I padded past her. Stopped. Changed my course and sat down.

She opened her eyes. Smiled. "You're home," she said. "Nice outfit."

I slipped off the hat. "I was at a party. A tacky dress-up party."

"So you went disguised as your father?"

"I was myself. I was pretending I was on safari."

"Was it fun?"

I shrugged. "It was . . . well . . . entertaining."

"Good."

A long silence followed. She continued to smile.

"Mom. Tell me again. What happens when we die?" I asked.

"We ascend to the next stage of existence. Shed our flesh. Become pure spiritual energy. We have so much more to do. To become."

"What if I don't believe that? What happens to me?"

"Your doubts are natural. All will unfold as it should."

I nodded. "That's good to know," I said.

I retired to my room. Everyone had an answer. But

I had none. I sighed. My lot, apparently, was to be an analyzer.

I went to my desk and recorded the day's events. Finally—arm tired, mind emptied—I collapsed on my bed and dreamed of jungles, tsetse flies and Elissa's warm hand.

eleven

SON OF THE NDEBELE

I was born in Saskatoon City Hospital at 11:05 P.M., August 19. My mother endured nine hours of labor and refused all medication. The attendees were a female doctor, two nurses, and Mom's midwife, Priscilla. I increased the population of the room, the city and the world by one.

I was also born at the same time fifteen thousand kilometers away in the district of Mpumalanga, South Africa. That's where my father was living with the Ndzundza, an Ndebele tribe. He had been there for six months, had heard of my mother's ever-swelling belly via letters.

Kgope, an old man of the tribe, burst into my father's conical mud house (there was also some dung mixed in as cement) and announced, "Unto you has son been born." It was 7:25 A.M. local time.

Dad was stunned. How did Kgope know? There were no phones. My father hadn't even spoken of the expected child.

Kgope explained: "My wife awoke. Shouted out 'Krep.' Then left our matrimonial bed and made this." He handed my father a Swazi tribal doll of cloth and beads. "It is gift. For you. It is called Krep. It is your son. Your son it is. He is Ndebele now. Protected by the ancestors."

He next presented Dad with a beer. Kgope was the best beer maker in the area. They drank and talked about the hopes my father had for me. When they were finished, Kgope stood, grabbed Dad's suitcase and began packing Dad's clothes.

"What are you doing?" Dad asked.

Kgope didn't stop. *"Ubaba makeze ekhaya,"* he said quietly.

It took Dad a moment to translate the words: *Father should come home.*

"Your son spoke to me. Through Krep. It is time for you to go."

And so he did. Dad came all the way home.

To see me.

His only son.

That was not the last of my connections with the Ndebele. Years later my father warned me about the cruelest physical stage all humans endure: puberty. He explained that manhood was a seed Mother Nature had planted inside me. When the time was right, it would grow out of my body. "It's nothing to be frightened of; we evolve. Never fear change."

I was ten. Holding a toy car in my hand, the metal cold against my palm.

Then he told me how the Ndebele take their pubescent males into the bush for two months, shave their heads, circumcise them and train them in the manly arts. This ritual is called the *wela*. When they return to the village, a celebration is held and they are admitted to the councils of men. As part of their training they learn a secret language in which words are spoken backward. This language may not be divulged to strangers, or even to their own women.

"It's a shame the West doesn't have any traditions like it," my father said. "Such an amazing sight, all those young men, their bald heads glistening in the sun. So proud." Dad promised to lead me through a Canadian version of the ritual upon his return. It would involve a trip to a northern lake, a fishing rod and sleeping bags. Luckily, I had already been circumcised.

"Even the most civilized mind needs rituals," Dad explained. "It soothes the primitive within."

He never got the chance to take me, but when puberty finally grew out of my body, I was unafraid. I knew I was an Ndebele youth taking that next inevitable step toward becoming a man.

About the same time, a doll arrived in the mail, from Kgope. Attached was a note in scribbled English: "Welcome to manhood, Krep."

Krep.

Perk.

A backward sign. A symbol.

I was a man now.

twelve

DREAM WORLD

At 7:50 A.M. our phone buzzed. Mom answered, talking in a hushed voice. A moment later, she padded into my room and presented a note. I read it groggily: *Session with Mr. Verplaz. 2:30 P.M.*

Mom's face was calm, except for the slightest downturn of her lips.

"I'll be there," I promised.

"I want to know why you weren't there yesterday."

"I—I forgot." Her demeanor indicated she needed more from me. "Mom, everything's so hectic at school. It's Grad Week. It's crazy! I honestly forgot."

"I would prefer if you didn't forget today."

I nodded. She didn't move. "You're too much like your father."

A chill skittered down my spine.

"You're in a dream world," she continued. "Not the real world. You've got to learn to stay grounded *and* dream. Let your spirit soar but remain in your body. Your father wandered too much in his own thoughts." She let out her breath. "You really should talk to him." Then she left.

I didn't move. She thought I was too much like Dad. I was worried I wasn't enough like him. I closed my eyes, pictured his face. I couldn't remember it perfectly, but I'd try to send him a message. Mom's orders. *Hey, Dad*, I thought. *Hello out there.* I wondered how long the message would take to reach him. *Ubaba makeze ekhaya. Pronto.*

Eventually, I got up. After a breakfast of oatmeal porridge soaked in soy milk, I marched toward my third-to-last day of school. The sun was in the east. Light that had traveled a hundred and fifty million kilometers in eight and a half minutes warmed my skin. A pleasant sensation.

Just as I caught sight of Groverly High, a wailing cacophony stopped me. The sound of thirty cats dying a slow death. Of the universe ripping apart.

Bagpipes. Somewhere nearby. The Scottish blood in my veins, from my mother's side, began to vibrate. My Celtic heart thudded with joy. I had no choice—I was genetically programmed to respond to that wailing. I followed the sound, heading toward the river.

The bagpiper was extremely good. He had to be part of a Highlander band. Or the army. I wondered if he'd be clad in full kilt, flame-red hair billowing in the breeze.

Dew dotted the grass. A few tails of mist curled around the edge of the river. A woman jogged past, weights attached to her wrists and ankles—her face set in a look of absolute determination. I strolled under the Victoria Bridge, turned. Froze.

There, above me on a knoll, was Delmar Brass. Clad in blue jeans and a black shirt, his long hair down, playing the pipes as if he'd just strolled off a Scottish ship. He was facing the river, blasting his song toward the high-rise buildings and hotels on the other side. The music stirred some ancient feeling in my body. Songs of my ancestors. A direct tonal connection to the past.

It tuned my biorhythms.

Watching Delmar, I was amazed at the revelation handed me. Two cultures exhibited in one person. Proof that we all came from the same tree.

There was also a lesson: Never make assumptions. Rely on observation, then make a conclusion.

I backed away and climbed up the hill. The bag-pipes slowly faded, but I still heard them echo inside my mind's ear. Groverly swallowed me readily. I sleep-walked down the halls and with numb fingers opened my locker. *Click.*

I stepped back, books in hand. Someone tripped over my leg and fell.

Marcia Grady was on the floor, looking up at me, blond hair perfectly coifed, lipstick expertly applied, a trace of blue shadow accentuating her eyes.

A face to fall in love with.

Mom was right. I was living in a dream world.

"Sorry," Marcia said as she gracefully got up off the floor. She was taller than me. "I didn't see you there."

"I too am sorry."

She smiled, her automatic reaction to everything. I knew why Willard had fallen in love with her: such innocence and beauty. Unattainable.

She picked up my books and handed them to me. "How are things going?"

"They progress," I answered. "In a good way, I

mean. Fine. Really." No one had ever told her that Willard had been in love with her. I wanted to say: Remember those phone calls where someone kept hanging up? That was Willard. But I bit my tongue. Better for her not to know. Still, in my mind Marcia and Willard were forever linked.

"Well," she said, "gotta go."

"Wait," I said. "Do you remember Willard?"

"Willard?"

"Willard Spokes. Will."

Her face showed no recognition. Then: sadness. "Oh . . . yes. He was the one who . . . yes. I remember him. He was a friend of yours, wasn't he?"

"A good friend," I said. "I—I just wanted to be sure people remembered him."

"I do. He was a quiet guy. A nice quiet guy."

I nodded. "Yes. He was."

"Well, see you," she said, walking away.

"Yes, in the future," I answered, watching her until she was lost in the crowd.

Memory. Somewhere in the coils of her brain Willard still existed.

thirteen

READING MAMMOTH ENTRAILS

"**R**eady for your 'igh tea, Perky?" Elissa asked in a faux British accent.

"I certainly am," I said. We'd decided to stroll around the schoolyard during break. Stopping at a set of old swings, we performed our impressions of human pendulums.

"I did some reading about this weird tea thing," she continued. "We learned it from the Brits. But we're mixed up, as usual. A high tea isn't a high-and-mighty, hoity-toity event. It really means 'It's high time we had a spot o' tea and something to eat.' " She dug her feet into the sand, stopping herself. "You're daydreaming again," she accused.

"I'm in the zone," I admitted. "Attuned to the potential of the universe. Just waiting for a revelation to hit."

"Or a truck," she said.

"Don't you have days like that?" I asked. "Where the world feels . . . unreal?"

"I worry about you," she said. "Every day is real for me."

"Never mind," I said. "Obviously my brilliance astounds you."

"You *are* in a different world," she teased. "I hope you can still tell time. The High Tea starts at four-thirty. Why don't we meet outside the school?"

"Sure," I said absently. "I'll be there."

We soon returned to our classes, learning nothing new. At precisely 2:27 P.M. I climbed the stairs to Groverly High's top floor, passing the soft-drink machine where Justin had threatened me. My shoulders tensed. By the fourth floor the tightness had doubled and my palms were moist. I breathed using my stomach muscles, aiming to restore calmness. I entered the fluorescent glow and squinted down the long, shadowy hallway.

It took considerable willpower to move my legs. As I got closer to the trapdoor, spittle gathered in my throat. I stopped underneath, mesmerized. How had Willard climbed to the roof? Had he moved a chair to this very spot? Had he used his opposable-thumbed hands to pull himself up?

A scratching came from the other side of the door. The hinges rattled. Then I noticed that the padlock was open.

Perspiration gathered on my forehead. "I remember," I rasped. An ice age came and went. "I remember you, Will."

One final long scratch.

I hurried on to Mr. Verplaz's office. On the door hung a sign:

All words spoken inside this room
will remain here.

It was intended to inspire trust, but I felt grief for all those trapped words. I wiped the cold sweat from my forehead and knocked.

"Come in," Mr. Verplaz said gently, sounding as if he were waking from a potent dream.

I opened the door to a closet-sized office. Mr. Verplaz sat behind an antique wooden desk, his hands touching in a gesture of prayer. He was a forty-year-old ascetic with tanned skin, a hawk nose and small, round-lensed glasses. His eyes were spectacular, the over-sized orbs of a well-groomed lemur, evolved to soak up moonlight.

School shaman. Truth seeker. Witch doctor.

"I said *come in,* Percival."

I closed the door and stepped over a collection of scrunched-up papers by the garbage can. His office hadn't changed since Willard's death. A forty-watt bulb still hung from the ceiling. The shade was pulled. Light bad. Darkness good. Where dreams come from. Folders lay scattered across his desk. A half-empty jar of lollipops sat precariously close to the edge. Books were piled on the floor. All a symbol of the chaos of the universe.

Mr. Verplaz pierced me with his mystical eyes. "Please sit down. It's good to see you."

I sat on the leather chair, which suddenly reclined at a sharp angle; I became an astronaut waiting to test gravity's bonds. We had walked on the moon. Our foot-prints would be there for millennia.

Pencils were stuck in the ceiling. When would one fall?

Mr. Verplaz cleared his throat. "Now, I'm not upset, but I'd like to understand why you missed yesterday's session."

"I . . . I forgot." I knew at once the shaman would recognize my statement as a lie. He surprised me with nodding acceptance.

"You are an exceptionally intelligent young man," he said quietly, as if letting me in on a great secret. "Do you know why you're here?"

"I was in a fight, so Groverly's patriarch ordered me to attend."

Mr. Verplaz smiled. "Are you angry with Mr. Michaels?"

"No."

"Then tell me, what is the real reason you are here?" This was another tool of *Homo shaman therapist*—a skin bag stuffed with questions.

"Apparently, the Teacher Tribe is concerned about my behavior."

"Do you understand why?"

"They are hired to assimilate me. It's their duty. Even if it is the last week of school."

"What's your favorite color?"

It took me a moment to process the question. "Gray."

"Why?"

"It's the color of the volcanic sediment surrounding Lucy's remains."

"Lucy?" He scratched his head, confused. I lost some respect for him.

"Yes, Lucy. *Australopithecus afarensis,*" I explained.

"Do you mean the ape fossil?"

"She was *not* an ape but an ancestor of humans. You are confusing her with the 'missing link' between ape and man. She is on *our* side of the divide. I'm surprised you're not aware of that."

The corners of his mouth curled into a grin. "You know a lot about human history, don't you?"

I nodded.

"What's the worst thing that's ever happened?"

"Ever?" I repeated. "Through all time?"

"Sure, all time."

"Easy. When *Australopithecus* climbed down from the trees and walked upright."

His smile disappeared. "Why?"

"Hiroshima."

"Explain."

I gathered my thoughts. The walls of this office would not be able to contain these words, but I decided to release them anyway. "In 1945 a crew of hominids piloted the *Enola Gay,* a B-29 bomber constructed by hominids. It carried a four-hundred-and-eight-kilogram atomic device built by another group of scientist hominids. They called the device Little Boy. They dropped this bomb on Hiroshima, a city full of Japanese hominids. Ten square kilometers were flattened: a hundred thousand unsuspecting hominids perished immediately. Another hundred thousand later succumbed to burns and radiation sickness."

Mr. Verplaz was speechless. He leaned forward, as though trying to get a clearer picture of me.

I continued. "Why didn't they flatten Mount Fujiyama instead? Wouldn't that have conveyed the same message? But they targeted Hiroshima, a city founded in the sixteenth century, then returned three days later and flattened Nagasaki. Just think of all the genetic lines—the years of evolution it took to create those specific human beings—all gone in a flash that reduced their DNA strands to nothing."

Mr. Verplaz had crossed his arms and shifted slightly away. I slid my chair closer.

"Pretend we could go back to that lush jungle where *Australopithecus afarensis Lucy* sits in a tree, minding her own business. What if we told Lucy that when she climbed down and stood upright, she would begin a process in which her offspring's offspring would climb into the cockpit of the *Enola Gay?* Would she stand upright? Or decide to stay in that tree for another five million years, leaving the world to the apes and chimpanzees?"

Mr. Verplaz adjusted his glasses. "So mankind doesn't deserve to exist?"

"It's not my job to judge."

"What is your job?"

"To observe. To take notes."

"For whom?"

For my father. Verplaz had nearly dragged the words out of me.

"For future anthropologists," I said carefully. His luminous, hypnotic eyes stared. He saw secrets. He truly was a shaman, descended from the great shamans who guided our tribes through dream worlds. I sensed his spirit surrounding me. I was in his bear cave.

"You were about to say something else."

I shook my head.

"How's your relationship with your mother?"

"She's loving, understanding and nurturing. And

I . . ." I wanted to use the word *love* but it was too vague, its meaning slippery. Instead: "I try to be a good son."

He loomed closer, now peering directly at me. His ancestors had once read mammoth entrails. His magico-religious powers were fine-tuned to the point of omni-science. "What about your father?" he whispered.

"He died long ago."

This startled Mr. Verplaz: He blinked and squinted at a paper, presumably the profile of Percival Montmount, Jr.

"Your father's dead?" the shaman said with disbelief. "I'm sure I would have read about it in the papers."

"I assure you, he has passed on."

"Are you comfortable talking about it?"

"Of course. Death is part of the life cycle. My father was bitten by a beetle in the Congo and infected with black Azazel sickness."

"A beetle bit him? Do they carry infections?"

"Did I say beetle? I'm mixing him up with Darwin." My thoughts were jagged, broken. "It was a tsetse fly."

"When did he die?"

"Three years ago."

"What kind of man was he? Warm? Aloof?"

I tapped my foot on the floor. Stopped. "He traveled frequently."

"Did you like him?"

"Of course. He was my father, I . . . I loved him. He was an excellent storyteller."

"What kind of stories?"

"About adventures in the field."

"Can you give me an example?"

I nodded eagerly. "Once, when my father was in New Guinea exploring some ruins, he found an ancient emerald ax used for sacrifices, a priceless, one-of-a-kind artifact that belonged to a long-extinct tribe. He knew this one discovery would bring him fame.

"He couldn't escape the thoughts of glory: He saw himself in front of the cameras gripping the sacrificial weapon. He set out to bring it home. For two nights he was plagued by nightmares, and on the third day he discovered he'd come full circle and was back at the ruins again. He tried heading in the opposite direction. Same result. Finally he restored the ax to its sacred place and was able to find his way back to civilization. He never told anyone but me about the ax."

Mr. Verplaz leaned on his elbows; the desk creaked. "Were your father's stories true?"

"What?"

"Did he tell the truth?"

"Of course." Anger had crept into my voice. "Of course," I repeated quietly.

"Are you on any meds?"

"No." My foot tapped hard now. Bipedal motion. Heel. Toe. Heel. Toe.

"I think you should see Dr. Skein. She's a psychiatrist. I hope you aren't offended by this suggestion."

"I would thoroughly enjoy the opportunity." Skein was another variation of his tribe. Her territory was the coiled layers of the brain.

The bell rang, indicating the end of our session, but Mr. Verplaz held me with a look. I wasn't sure what he wanted. Finally he dismissed me with a nod. Partway out the door I stopped, realizing I had a spiritual question for him: "Have you ever heard a voice in the school attic?"

"What kind of voice?" he asked, clearly alarmed.

"Oh, nothing," I said, stepping out the door. I closed it behind me.

All words spoken inside this room will remain here.

The statement was false. The words Mr. Verplaz and I had shared buzzed around my head like dragonflies over some Mesozoic swamp. I walked quickly under the trapdoor and down the stairs. The school was deserted, but the students' pheromones and discarded skin cells clung to the walls. The buzzing words followed me home and into my room.

Then: I forced them out through my pen in perfect order. The day's events. Observations. Interpretations.

There was a knock at my window. I ignored it. It became more insistent. I carried on with my work. I missed the Graduation High Tea and the accompanying rituals. My article took precedence.

Later I grew vaguely aware that my mother was sitting on my bed in the lotus position.

"Perk?" she said.

I kept writing.

"Perk, what are you doing?"

"I'm trying to finish an article."

"Are you okay?"

"I am feeling incredibly self-actualized, Mom. Top-o'-the-world, in fact."

I jotted down another sentence.

"Will you please stop?"

"When I'm finished," I informed her.

I'm not certain when she left.

Sooner than I expected it, morning light brightened my room. It was important to keep writing. At last the words quit buzzing in my ears and I slept. After four hours I woke up, my mind precise. Focused. Omniscient.

fourteen

THE PRIMITIVE WITHIN

I waited for Elissa in the center of what used to be our front lawn, seated cross-legged on top of Ogo, a giant rock. Three years ago Mom had terra-formed this square space into a rock garden, ripping out the lawn, while feeling guilt over the death of every blade. She then brought home stones from her various spiritual trips, planting them alongside the rosebushes, vines and sunflowers. The stones had been infused with ancient spirits, so she'd asked each one its permission to bring it here.

Ogo was the biggest. And the most benevolent, according to Mom. He was the protector of our lawn, with a thousand years of wisdom in his igneous form. He also made a great chair.

The hair on my arms shot up. The streetlight began to hum, then flicked on, heralding the evening. Elissa's black VW bug pulled up and stopped. Synchronicity. Of course.

I couldn't see her through the darkened windows. The car had been a gift from her parents on her seventeenth birthday. She prized it second only to Fang, though she felt guilt about the carbon monoxide it produced.

I untangled my legs and walked over and tugged on

95 ⭐

the door handle. It was locked. I knocked on the window. Nothing. Knocked again. *Click.* I opened the door, slid inside.

Elissa jammed on the gas and I slammed the door. She glared ahead as I struggled to fasten my seat belt.

"You're in a hurry," I commented.

She flicked a bit of fluff off her black baseball shirt. Her chest and back were decorated with a stylized ankh. The shirt was from Logoless—a company that designed clothing for modern activists. She'd ordered it online. "Where were you yesterday?" she finally said. "And today, for that matter?"

"I decided not to attend school," I answered, pressing a button that let my window down a crack; the effluvia of the traffic swept inside.

"You skipped the second-last day of Grade Twelve? What's the point of that?"

"I was working on my book."

She refused to even glance at me. Her mauve lipstick accentuated the thickness of her lips. Her favorite eyebrow ring with the tiny dragonfly glinted in the streetlight; sandalwood perfume drifted from her body. She smelled friendly but didn't look it.

We passed through the final set of lights before Saskatoon's outskirts. Vehicles of all descriptions stretched in front of us like giant manic crustaceans, speeding around the edge of the city and into the wilderness. We were navigating toward the River Party, the most primitive of all Grad celebrations.

A Mustang, its tires augmented to the point of parody, roared past, rear end swerving, horn blaring. Two males waved muscular arms out the window. The vehicle drove down the wrong side of the highway, then veered into the proper lane, dodging an oncoming truck.

The Highway Tribe. A short-lived species.

A kilometer later Elissa turned onto a gravel road, following the line of cars. "I knocked at your window. I saw you sitting at your desk."

"I don't remember that."

"That's funny. You looked up, then ignored me."

"Elissa, I didn't hear you. I was having an intense experience, writing an article about . . ." Now, what was the topic? "Well, I didn't mean to ignore you."

"You shut me out. That's the point."

"I am sorry. Very sorry. I just had to get my work done."

She nodded solemnly. We rattled along the road, trees forming a wall on either side. I leaned back in my seat, appreciating the insectlike elegantness of her VW bug; it was as though we were riding inside a hollowed-out bumblebee, engine buzzing.

A tiny plastic skeleton hung from the rearview mirror, jaws clacking with every bump. I gazed in awe at its bipedal feet, examined the opposable thumbs. What if we had evolved to the size of this toy? It would have been so much better for the planet. We'd inhabit one sixth of the space, our tiny anthill cities just dots across the world. Coyotes would control our population.

The VW bug glided over a rise and there it was: the river. An open view of black water, three giant bonfires along the edge, revelers dancing between them. A flashback to the primitive within; a return to the life-giving waters where our ancestors first built their tiny mud-hut communities. Tonight's celebration was about the most basic elements: fire, water, earth and air.

And beer. A cornucopia of brewed fermented barley. I wondered if it was to honor the memory of the two Groverly students killed while driving drunk last year. A libation to their hovering spirits.

The segmented line of cars disassembled, finding parking spots next to bushes along the road. Members of all tribes rushed exuberantly toward the bonfires.

Elissa guided the bug to the edge of the ditch and stopped. "We're here," she announced quietly, turning off the car. The dashboard lights went black. She let out a huff of air, indicating continuing emotional turmoil.

I glanced out the window as a swarm of teens streamed past. The riverbank teemed with life. Action. Interaction. There was so much to observe. I clutched the door latch, but Elissa wouldn't budge.

"When will you show me your field journal?" she asked.

"When it's *absolutely* ready."

"Don't bite my head off!"

Had I sounded that angry? "I—I want it to be perfect before I release it to the world," I explained. "You understand that, don't you? It's my life's work."

"Life's work?" She hugged herself. Her V collar displayed her clavicle. "You're seventeen, Percy. How can you have a life's work?"

I shrugged. Elissa pointed at the bonfires. "This is our final night as high school students. We should try to enjoy it."

She'd chosen a different topic, at least. "Yes, graduation," I agreed, "ascension to a higher order. To the next stage. We are pupae waiting for the end of chrysalis."

"What do we change into?"

"We?"

"Yes, you and I. What do we become?" she asked. The moonlight made her lips glisten.

"Nothing. It's the other tribes' task to change. Ours is to observe."

She went quiet again, ruminating heavily. "Don't you ever get sick of watching?"

"What?"

"It . . . well, it used to be a joke between us. All this anthro stuff."

"It's my . . . *our* job. Come on, Elissa. Let's observe—join the party. Have fun, like we did when Will was here."

Will's name had popped out. Just like that. Elissa's eyes teared up. "Do you think he's watching us now? From somewhere up there?"

This was not the time for me to get into my theories about the statistical chances of life after death. "Maybe he is. And he's giving us the thumbs-up. Doing his best *Planet of the Apes* impression."

She breathed in, steeled herself and opened her door. "Let's party, then."

But now I was frozen. This talk had resurrected the memory of Elissa holding me in my room after Will's funeral as tears slid down my face and she said again and again, "Everything will be fine."

"What are you waiting for?" Elissa had come around to my side of the car. "I thought you were ready for this."

"Thank you," I whispered.

"What?" she said. "Come on."

As we strolled to the river, flames from the fires licked the sky, lighting everyone's faces. Sparks scattered through the air as the wood crackled. Teens gyrated, hypnotized by the blaze. One Grunge Tribe member sucked in smoke from a joint and gazed at the moon with rapture. Was he a shaman divining the inner workings of the universe? About to announce the ultimate human dream quest? He coughed, releasing a smoggy cloud. Then he pressed one nostril closed and blew onto the ground, giggling.

"This *is* kind of amazing," Elissa said as we meandered through the crowd, the tribes dancing around us in a majestic celebration. All differences were forgotten, boundaries erased; tonight they were one, on the edge of their new lives.

Music pounded out of hidden speakers, rhythmic chanting against the beating of drums. My father had once penetrated the deepest, darkest heart of the jungle and discovered two tribes dancing and singing together. They had stopped their celebration to gape at him, believing he was a god.

So many stories. Night after night, by my bedside. Then he was gone, never to be seen again.

My eyes ached. I stumbled over a broken branch, nearly fell.

"You okay, Percy?" Elissa asked.

"The smoke. It stings."

She took my hand and led me away from the fire. There were other tribes occupying the hinterland, hiding from the light: the Necking Tribe, the Smoker Tribe, the Cool and Detached Tribe. We stepped around abandoned blankets and zigzagged between overturned lawn chairs and entwined bodies. We found a spot where we could be alone and stared back at the distant flames.

What was it like that first time a human saw fire? Were we mesmerized by the power inside that flickering?

"It's all too weird," Elissa said. "Like they're dancing while the world ends."

There was a clink. A pop. Then she pushed a cold bottle into my hand.

"What's this?" I asked.

"Beer. It was sitting right here. A gift from the gods, obviously."

"But I can't consume beer."

"Why?"

I squinted at the bottle. "It will affect my judgment."

"It'll loosen you up. Don't tell me you still haven't tried it."

"I won't."

She chuckled. "Not even a sip? Aren't you curious?"

"No."

"Think of it as a tribal potion," she whispered, so close her breath tickled my ear hairs. "You can't experience the tribe's inner world without this elixir. Just a swig. Besides, you need to relax."

She drank from hers, so I followed suit, feeling the cool glass on my lips and swallowing quickly. The beer was cold; the liquid entered my stomach with gusto. I had the momentary feeling it would all come gurgling back up my esophagus. Coughing, sputtering, I said, "People enjoy this? It's like ginger ale and vinegar."

"They adapt to it—that's what humans do. Adapt. It gets better."

Elissa swigged from her bottle; I mimicked her. The odor was putrid. Which tribesperson had mixed water with rotted grains and risked a sip? And then convinced other unsuspecting hominids to partake? I took another long gulp.

"You like it." She handed me another. "It's my new job to get you to loosen up. I'm the leopard queen of the Loosen-Up Tribe."

We sat on a big log, a good decision because I felt dizzy. The potion's essence was bringing out my inner Cro-Magnon. The pounding music. The smoke. I had established a link with my past. There was a driving force pushing all organisms forward, out of the water, always ahead, compelling us to survive, to become stronger, faster, better able to conquer our environment. I was channeling it now.

Elissa patted my knee. "You're pretty quiet. What are you thinking?"

"About everything." The words slid out. "About you. Me. Everything."

She took this as an invitation to move closer. I hadn't noticed how cool it had become. The heat of her body: comforting.

"I really do care about you," she said.

My arm was around her, though I couldn't recall positioning it there. My mind went blank. She turned toward me and I mirrored her. Her breath was tainted with beer, but it wasn't nauseating. We were from the same tribe, watching our ancestors dance.

She leaned forward and we pressed our lips together.

I had never kissed before. This seemed fated: From

the moment my cells formed, they'd been programmed to find her lips and kiss them.

She slid her tongue into my mouth. An ancient feeling: our tongues moving in a warm, moist place like the pool in which life first formed.

Elissa sighed. "That's nice," she whispered. I kissed her again and my hand explored her back, tracing each vertebra. It felt absolutely natural. To caress. Explore. I slid my hand under the front of her shirt and cupped my fingers over her left breast, using my opposable thumb to squeeze. She pressed closer.

I sighed, then spoke gently into her ear. "So this is what the female mammae feel like."

Elissa jerked as if she'd been stung. *"What?"*

My hand was frozen.

"What?" she repeated, sitting back. My hand slipped from her, fell onto my lap. "Is that all I am? An experiment? Another study?"

I opened my mouth: no words. My thoughts were caught in amber. Finally, I blurted out, "I was just remarking on the experience."

"Oh, Jesus!"

"Oh, Jesus what?" I asked.

"Is that what you were doing? Just observing my mammae? My mammae!" She crossed her arms, covering Mother Nature's gift. Her face was a pattern of shadows. The firelight glinted in her eyes. "You don't live, do you, Percy. You just record."

"I . . . I do my job."

"Your job? It was your job to feel me up?"

"I . . . I don't know."

"You don't live!"

"I do so!"

"You don't *live*. There's a big difference. God, I shouldn't have to explain it. I don't want you to touch me for the first time and just think how you'll write it in your stupid journal. I want you to *be* here."

"I . . . I was . . ."

"I'm tired of doing what we do. All the fake studies. The staring. It's not normal."

Elissa stood and looked down at me. "Your father didn't die in the Congo, Percy. Why can't you tell the truth?"

"I did tell the truth! A tsetse fly bit him. He died of black Azazel sickness."

"I don't believe you."

"He did. I swear it's the truth." I could remember the *National Geographic* reporter coming to our door bawling her eyes out, her long blond hair undone. Mom not letting her in. It had happened.

Elissa glared. "I'm going home." Her tone was cool. "I'll give you a ride."

I couldn't move. I couldn't speak. I shook my head.

"Fine, then. And I won't be going to Grad with you. I might not go at all." She paused for a microsecond. "Goodbye, Percy."

fifteen

SAME TREE

Temporal confusion.
Time had passed.
Amount: unknown.
One hour? Two?
I clutched a bottle. Empty. I opened my hand. The bottle floated down, crashed in slo-mo against its brothers. The bonfires raged, sparks shot into the sky— flaming moths. Dying galaxies. Shadows danced madly to a bass beat. Distorted guitars grinding like tectonic plates.

The fire beckoned. I stood, took a step, stumbled, fell. The contents of my stomach lurched, so I clamped my mouth shut, used a tree to pull myself up. What had happened to my feet? It felt as though I were walking through clay. Would future anthropologists gaze in wonder at my hardened footprints? I staggered past prone hominids, some with faces pressed together. Others sat cross-legged, mesmerized by the fire. The flames were higher than before, their heat making my cells dance.

I tried to enter the crowd that surrounded one of the

bonfires. I wanted to see the center of the circle of flames. The core. An evolutionary secret I had been denied was there. Maybe the teachings the Ndebele youth learned during their manhood rites.

I fell, putting my hands out too late. My jaw struck the ground. Time oozed. Then the pain hit; my eyes watered. I got up, wiping my face.

I tried to break through at a different place. A male pushed me away, his face blurry. The square jaw and short hair reminded me of Justin. It had to be him, or one of his brethren.

"*Gigantopithecus blacki,*" I slurred. "Species died out. They did."

"Bug off, Einstein!"

"I'm Darwin!" I insisted. "Darwin!"

"Okay, Darwin! Go puke somewhere else."

Vomiting? The mere mention of it awakened gastrointestinal turmoil. I stumbled, turned away from the flame and bent over a log, and my digestive system flowed backward.

"Hey, whazzat," the log said, despite its lack of a larynx. "Oh, Jesus, get away!" Something flew out of the dark, a foot, a fist, a bottle, striking me in the chest.

My eyes stung. I weaved toward the circle of bodies. They were hominids. I was a hominid. We had the same number of fingers, the same number of chromosomes. They would let me enter the inner circle. I wanted to see the flames close up.

I tripped and fell into a group of shadows.

"Aw, back off!" one said, shoving me away. "He's coated in puke." I was pushed again, so that I rolled over into a puddle of mud.

In the past now. Long ago.

Three First Nations males looked down at me. Two large. One bald and thin as a colt. Flickering flames sharpened their features.

Was this pre-Columbian times? Had I crossed the Bering Strait?

The thin one kicked the ground, and dirt clumps smacked the side of my face. "Get out of here—go on."

I held up my hands. "The buffalo are all gone—the bison, I mean."

"What?" a larger lump barked. "What did you say?"

"I didn't kill them," I explained quickly. "The slaughter wasn't my fault. And the Beothuks, I understand how they felt."

"Understand this!" the thin one hissed. "Shove off, whitey!" He stepped toward me.

"Wait," the third one said. He moved into the light. "That you, Percy?" A familiar visage. Young face. Ancient eyes. Delmar Brass.

"Yes. Yes. It is I."

"What are you doing?"

"Elissa left. She left. Left. Left."

They stared quizzically at me.

"You know this guy?" The thin one pointed.

"Yeah," Delmar answered, "I do."

I needed to explain the link between us. "We come from the same tree," I began. "All of us climbed down from the same tree. All skin colors are mutations of our original color. *Australopithecus* is inside everyone. Witness Lucy. We come from the same tree."

Delmar chuckled. "Yeah, we come from the same tree. That's right, buddy. Don't get yourself all riled up. I see."

"You see what?" the skinny one said. "He's drunk."

"How much did you drink?" Delmar asked.

"A vast quality. Quantity. Five beers."

"Five beers?" The thin one again. "That's all it took to get you to barf? What kind of . . ."

I blacked out. When I opened my eyes again, I was on my back, squinting up, and Delmar was hovering over me, laughing. I giggled. Maybe this was a vision quest. I'd need to find an animal spirit. I thought of an owl, but its large eyes only reminded me of Elissa.

"She went away," I announced. "She left. Left. Left me here. Flew away."

Oh, wait. I'd said that already.

"I'll give you a ride home," Delmar said.

"Just let him sleep it off here," whined the thin one. "He'll be fine."

"No. I have to." Delmar paused, scratched his chin and chuckled. "We come from the same tree."

He helped me up and guided my unresponsive body to an old, dented truck. The interior smelled of sweet grass. Or maybe the scent emanated from the Marilyn Monroe deodorizer on the rearview mirror. Her shape drew my attention, her dress blown up to reveal her famous limbs. So smooth. The engine roared. Delmar jammed the truck into gear. Marilyn wiggled.

Beauty. Beauty and evolution. A connection. Somehow.

I pressed my face against the window. The coolness felt good. The bonfires disappeared. Delmar cranked the radio and a rock song about love tumbled out.

"You play a mean bagpipe," I said.

"Thanks. Always did like the sound. Gets my heart pumping."

We are one, I thought. *We are all one.* I closed my eyes. When I opened them, we were home.

"You ever get that article published?" he asked.

"Still trying." Both words were a struggle. "*National Geographic* next. Or *Modern Science.* Someone will take it."

"Keep on keeping on."

I have to, I wanted to say. We all must keep on. Then I leaned on the heavy door and stumbled out, and he sped off. I slouched across the lawn and crawled through my window, shedding mud all over my bedroom.

sixteen

NDEBELE RETURN

My bladder was a giant, expanding zeppelin.

I woke up in the middle of the night with one desperate need. I blink-walked to the bathroom, relieved myself, then cranked open the sink tap. The first blast of H_2O was rust-stained, but I didn't hesitate. I drank deeply. A lost desert nomad at the oasis.

My brain expanded/contracted/expanded. Painfully. Some scientists say that if the spaces between everything were collapsed, the universe could be condensed into a cantaloupe-sized object. Not a grand watermelon or royal pumpkin: a measly cantaloupe. They suggest that was the dimension of the universe before the Big Bang. Well, another universe was inside my skull, rushing to obliterate the present.

I put my lips to the tap and gulped again. Looked into the mirror. Mud stained my face, a charcoal streak blackened my brow. *Australo-ugly-Percy-ithecus.* Sobering up stripped layers from my humanity. Desapienization. Soon I would be reduced to grunting.

Elissa didn't want to go to Grad with me.

We hate you, Percival.

I had clouded my anthropological eyes with alcohol and succumbed to imitating their behavior. I did not need a mate. I did not need them. I had to stay pure and prepare for the next great revelation. The Yanomamo call themselves *waiteri*. It means fierce. From now on I'd be *waiteri* in the pursuit of my goal.

I doused my face. My mind remained foggy. Embrangled. I needed something else. I thought of the Ndebele rite of passage. I dug in the drawer, grasped a pair of scissors. I clipped and cut, dropping hair into the sink.

I reached for the razor.

seventeen

REBORN

Mom examined me from her side of the breakfast table. When I'd first sat down she'd displayed shock, but like a stone dropped in the ocean, that shock sank below the surface. Placidity ruled.

She set down her tea. "So this is your last day as a high school student."

"Yes."

"And you've chosen rebirth?"

I spread almond butter across my toast. The pungent scent drifted up and my stomach tightened. I forced a bite. Masticated. "I am not sure what you mean, Mom."

"Why did you shave your head?"

I palmed my smooth skull. It was hot. The coils of my brain blazed and every razor nick tingled. My fingers were cool, which was comforting because my head ached. My first hangover; I would make notes later.

"I . . . uh . . ." The reasons had been lucid last night. Now: vague. Something to do with the Ndebele

manhood rites. Krep. Krep. My thoughts conglomer-
ated slowly. "It. Was. A. Dare," I said finally. "A dare."

"Who dared you?"

"Elissa."

A frown flickered across my mother's lips. Disbelief and anger nearly gained a foothold, but the placid
look won.

She stared at me. I ate. A memory spilled out my
lips. "Did Cindy Mozkowski come to our door?"

Mom turned pale. "When?"

"Three years ago. To tell us . . . about Dad. Was
she here? Crying?"

"I've only seen *her* once. At the airport. Why are
you asking this?"

"I. Just. I seem to have mixed up a memory of her.
That's all. Nothing." I looked down at my toast.

"Your father is coming tonight."

I shivered. "Oh," I said. "Oh." I hadn't committed
to an emotion. Then I felt it. Impossible. The genitor—
father—would *not* be there. His body had been reduced to its basic elements. "Will he float down from
heaven, Mom? Rise up from the Netherworld? Rein-
carnate as a butterfly and flip-flap through the ceremony? Will I wear him as a brooch?"

"Why are you so mad, Perk?"

A primordial anger soup boiled inside my skull.
"We go back to the earth. That's the way of things."

"What are you talking about?"

I stood up. "Why do people keep asking that? No
one ever knows what I'm talking about. What it
means. No one! Stupid, stupid hominids."

"Percy, what is it?"

I shook my head. How could I explain everything from *Australopithecus afarensis* to modern man? "It's nothing. Absolutely nothing."

Then I pulled my backpack off its hook on the wall and banged the door shut behind me.

eighteen

LITTLE BANG

Let's begin at the beginning. The real beginning. The early universe had ten billion and one protons created for every ten billion antiprotons. What's the big deal about that extra proton? Simple. Without it, matter and antimatter would have destroyed each other and there wouldn't have been a universe.

After the Big Bang there had to be exactly enough matter to clump into planets and stars, but not so much that it would all be pulled back together by gravity into the cantaloupe. The sun had to burn at least three and a half billion years to aid the creation of life. The earth had to rotate the perfect number of degrees from the sun, have enough gravity to hold an atmosphere, and the proper conditions to produce water. Only then could life begin. Without any of these factors, you get *nada.* Nil. Zero. No sane sentient being would bet on life forming on the third planet.

Which made it a miracle that I was at the front doors of Groverly High for my final day of Grade Twelve. I strode inside, head erect, eyes darting back and forth, eager to capture every significant event. A few students stared at my new visage—a Back-to-Buddha look. Most ignored me, including Elissa, whom I twice glimpsed in the hallway. She didn't even glance in my direction.

There were no classes, only a final goodbye from each teacher. Some classmates exchanged gifts or cards with each other, but I didn't receive anything. I report this to keep the facts straight. I felt no envy.

After lunch my peers dressed for photographs. I declined since I didn't want my soul sucked into the camera. I would forever be remembered in the yearbook as "no picture available."

There was a break between school and the graduation banquet. I went home, retreated silently to my room and wrote in my field journal. I scrutinized my words until my stereoscopic eyes ached.

"You're here," Mom said, entering my room without knocking. "Did you go to the banquet?"

"I didn't have time."

"Time?" She paused. "I hope you're not mad because I decided not to go. I—I just couldn't be in the same room as all that roast beef. You know that."

"I'm not angry. I missed it for my own reasons."

"Are you feeling better? This morning you were so upset."

"I was tired. That's all. There's so much to do." I looked at my watch. "I have to get dressed; the ceremony's going to start soon."

"I'd better get ready too. I found the perfect outfit at Value Village." On her way out my door she added, "Your father will hate it, though."

Dad, again? I thought. *Just let it go, Mom.*

I clad myself in the gray suit she'd purchased at the Salvation Army. It was too small for my frame. Had I grown overnight? I clipped on my tie and slipped into a pair of black herbivore-hide dress shoes.

Mom met me at the door in a white robe that only a Vulcan would wear. She straightened the shoulders of my suit and let out a sigh. "You look beautiful, Percy. I can't believe you're graduating."

"Me either, Mom," I said, quickly kissing her cheek. Then I ran the three blocks to school.

The recently assembled Grad Tribe was in a hallway near the back of the stage. Various females had caked their features with makeup and preserved their hair with gel and spray. Males stood uncomfortably in their new suits, hands in pockets, tugging ties, inspecting their shoes as if trying to recall why they weren't wearing sneakers.

I approached the sign-in desk. Ms. Nystrom looked up, frowned.

"You're late, Percy."

"I am aware of my tardiness," I answered. "It was unavoidable. It won't happen again, I promise." I winked. Her face was blank. "Get it? School's finished so I won't be back, therefore I can't be late."

"Yes, that is funny," she replied flatly. "I'll miss your sense of humor."

I thought of all the times she'd indulged me in class when I'd expounded on my theories regarding literature and evolution. She deserved a final gift, so I offered, "A birthmark on the left cheek is a sign of intelligence and good luck in Thai culture."

She looked up, eyes guarded. Then: a slight smile, making her birthmark crease together. "Good luck to you, Mr. Montmount," she said, handing me a graduation gown. I slung it over my arm and joined the crowd, amused that the males would submit to such effeminate dress.

Clusters of visibly nervous students chatted hesitantly, straightening each other's gowns and fixing their tresses like monkeys hunting for head lice. I retrieved my field notebook and jotted notes.

No Elissa sightings. No surprise. We were packed in the hallway like lab rats in a cage. The masses parted for the walking monolith, Justin. He lumbered through the students, his robe draped over one shoulder, *Gigantopithecus blacki* on a mission. He paused to inspect me; his eyes revealed no warmth, no anger, just contentment—an odd expression on his square-jawed face. Graduation agreed with him; maybe he'd won a football scholarship.

"Bald is beautiful," he said. "You look like one of them Shaolin kung fu fighters. Pretty gutsy to shave your head for Grad."

I blinked. Was that a compliment? He waited for a reaction from me. I tried not to send signals of fear or antagonism.

"Do you have any plans for next year?" he asked. I was stunned; he wanted to converse. I remained silent, alert. At first he grimaced, then—a grin. "Happy graduation, Montmount," he said without a hint of malice, clapping me on the shoulder. Was graduation like the so-called afterlife in which forgiveness was offered to all? Or did the suit somehow make him transcend into maturity?

"Thank you," I said. "Same sentiments to you."

He gave me the thumbs-up and turned away. I stared after him until he was swallowed by the river of dark robes.

I found a corner and wrestled into my robe, a butterfly struggling to reenter a cocoon. As the gown slipped over my bare-skinned skull, something in me changed, as though each brain cell were suddenly imprinted with new understanding. I had accessed a secret layer of my corpus callosum, the site of intuition known to mystics and the greatest scientists. Eureka zone! My eyes focused perfectly. I looked down at the gown and saw the stitches a hominid had designed and bequeathed to mankind. A pattern within a pattern.

The graduates had coagulated into groups. Did an inner impulse draw them together like one-celled organisms? A genetic program passed to us by the amoebae?

I was on the edge of ascertaining this knowledge when the loudspeaker barked: "Ladies and gentlemen, please line up in the hall according to your last names."

Several teachers held up placards. I found M–P.

The line ahead of me had morphed. An apelike creature was at the beginning, followed by a slightly taller one. The next had wider shoulders, a straighter stance, then a fourth and fifth, each taller than the rest, still dressed in gowns. A vision. A reward. A teacher grunted and the line advanced. As each hairy graduate passed through the portal, we drew closer to the beginning of our own evolution. Step by inexorable step, I moved toward it too. What would be on the other side? I passed through, brain tingling.

The stage was lit like a football stadium. We shuffled across the gym floor, up the stairs and into the glare.

Several older tribes stared—fathers, mothers, grandparents, all witnesses to this ancient ceremony. We would be their replacements, the next batch of genetic material that superseded them. Our job would be to carry the human race forward for another generation.

Their eyes examined and measured. My naked skull buzzed, felt each molecule of air. We took our places, settling into seats set on risers. I spotted Elissa, her face hard as a Sphinx's.

The ritual began with Principal Michaels delivering a glorious oration to send us into the future. Time. Cut. Away. I snapped to attention for the valedictorian speech: our *über-teen*. A female who waxed on about how we would fulfill our biological destinies.

The principal returned to the mike, spoke solemnly, his words so deep they were garbled. But I caught the last few: ". . . a moment of silence for Willard Spokes."

I swallowed and glanced behind me at the *S* section. There was an empty chair for Willard. They had honored him. The silence lasted a lifetime. Then the spell was broken when a female yelled: "Willard rocked!"

Elissa. Everyone gawked at her, until someone began clapping: Marcia Grady. The graduates, then the audience joined in.

When the noise died down, Michaels spoke again. An invitation. One by one we descended to the stage to receive our totems. Justin was one of the first. He brandished his diploma as if he'd pulled a sword out of a stone. The crowd applauded. A few graduates later, another Jock Tribe member repeated the gesture and was met with half the response. Student after student accepted diploma after diploma. Delmar walked up smiling, hair tied back. Somewhere in the crowd his mother made a *hi-ni-ni* sound. Several others repeated it. Marcia Grady soon followed, looking absolutely beautiful. If only Willard could have experienced this moment. I glanced back at his empty chair.

Then: Elissa. She walked slowly across the stage, gown flowing around her. A priestess in a solemn ceremony, she wore no makeup, no jewelry, and her hair was tied back. When she took her diploma I expected some symbolic action, perhaps defiance. Instead, she joined the line.

Soon my name was announced.

The voice of Fate. I advanced to Principal Michaels, who guarded the triangular pile of rolled diplomas. Three steps led up to the platform. I climbed using a system of flesh, blood, reflexes and nerves that had taken millions of years to evolve.

Then it hit me. I was genetically programmed to die. Nature's tidy system: We expire so we don't compete with our children. The faster we produce offspring, the faster our species mutates into something better adapted to the environment. I was next in line. One day I would be sitting in that crowd, watching my replacements. Would their feet be webbed?

I stepped onto the platform. A spotlight nearly blinded me. I extended my opposable-thumbed right hand to receive the holy paper. *Australopithecus afarensis* reaching for a bone that would become a tool.

FLASH.

Neurons fired too rapidly to comprehend. Applause thundered as I grasped the scroll. And suddenly . . .

FLASH.

I saw all history. From the beginning of the universe to now, condensed into shining moments. The earth forming. The first movement of life. The rise of vertebrates. Dinosaurs. Mammals. Man painting his cave walls. Aztec priests cutting open the chests of prisoners of war and wrenching out their beating hearts, holding them to the sky. The Romans burning Carthage, gas flooding an Auschwitz chamber. Japanese hominids lifting their eyes, pupils dilated by a hydrogen flash, then my father leaving my mother for the woman with blond hair, leaving me for . . .

Wait.

That.

Was not.

A historical fact.

FLASH.

The crowd of hominids came into focus. Became individuals. There was my mother with her Mona Lisa smile. Beside her. Someone else. A hand raised in a half wave. A man.

My father.

Percival Montmount, Sr.

A glowing blue ghost. Waving.

I turned toward him. Stepped from the line of evolution into the brilliant light.

"Dad," I whispered. Then I was falling, pushing aside a chair. Falling off the stage, down into darkness.

My body felt something (pain?) but maybe just a harsh jarring.

Voices. "Are you all right?"

My mother knelt beside me.

My father? Gazing at me? Light beginning to glow.

"Want your eyes back?" I whispered.

"Whu-what?"

"Taking? Your eyes back now?"

Then blackness.

nineteen

AWARENESS

The heat was unbearable. The smoke so thick my eyes watered, and the scent of burning sweet grass permeated every molecule of air. I was shirtless, sweating exponentially, my body quickly becoming a shell.

Gray Eyes sat across from me, the bucket of fire-heated rocks between us. He pulled out what looked like a bull's horn and sprinkled water across them. Steam rose, hissing. He sat back. He hadn't spoken for the last twenty minutes. He'd built the sweat lodge this morning, at my mother's request. She sat to my right, eyes closed. Clad in white, her hair stringy and wet, her legs crossed. She too had been silent, not even an *omm* to interrupt this afternoon sweat.

The door, covered by blankets and a tarp, faced east, toward the rising sun, the rising of wisdom. The Sioux, whom Mom sometimes emulated, saw the inside of the lodge as the womb of Mother Earth, the darkness as ignorance, the stones as the arrival of life and the hissing steam as the creative forces of the universe becoming active. The fire represented eternity.

They'd explained all this to me after I crawled inside, then told me to forget it. To dwell on the symbols would only lead to confusion. The sweat would purify me.

I closed my burning eyes, and that made them feel better. Behind them, vague memories. My arm ached. I'd fallen from the stage last night. My mother had guided me home to bed, where I'd slept deeply. When I awoke she dragged me to the table, fed me tofu soup, the best I'd ever had. A quintessential stomach heater. Then I was brought here to the sweat lodge. Willingly.

Wait. There was something else. I'd seen my father, too.

Alive.

"Percy," Mom whispered.

I opened my eyes. "Yes."

"Where are you?" she asked.

"Here. Right here."

She smiled. "Good. Gray Eyes and I will leave you alone now. It's time."

"Alone?"

"Yes. With your thoughts. With you. It will only be for twenty minutes. But it might seem longer."

I nodded.

They crawled out the front, lifting the flap to reveal a fire, just a few meters from the tent. Tiny tongues of flame licked red embers, and inside that heat were several rocks. Gray Eyes returned a moment later carrying two more rocks on a forked stick. He dropped them into the pail and handed me the water horn with a wink.

Then: alone. Me and my thoughts. But what was I

supposed to think about? The universe was too complex to comprehend. The last few days, months, years—even more complex. So I tried not to think of anything.

That worked for a microsecond.

Earlobes. That's what came to mind. Elissa's. The half-moon shape, the way she always wore some new, interesting earrings that jangled when she laughed.

Her laugh. High-pitched and from the belly. Her presence filled the lodge. I wept hard, struggling to muffle my sobs.

When I gained control of myself again, my mind's eye conjured an acne-scarred afterimage: Willard, smiling at me. It was as if I were staring at a cave painting, a message from an ancient time.

Where there's a Will, there's a way.

His voice. Speaking to me. The hissing of steam off the rocks. Then he was gone. Returned to sender.

I ached to talk with him again. And Elissa. The three of us together. But he was beyond us now, in his own universe.

I'd been still for too long. I had to move; I sprinkled the rocks and was enveloped in fresh steam. Time expanded inside this room. How long had it been since my mother had left?

The tribes had dispersed. Justin, Marcia, all the teachers: gone. Graduation over and summer would swallow them. No longer would we walk the same hallways, breathe the same air, attend the same classes. Other students would fill Groverly, but I would have no connection with them.

Good. It was time to find new connections. New feelings.

An eon passed. My thoughts returned to the beginning.

I was suddenly at show-and-tell in Grade One, holding up a shrunken head, explaining to the class that it was from faraway Afreeka, a hot place. The head was from a white hunter whom the witch doctors had caught. I went into details: First they dismembered him, then severed his neck with cleavers. The teacher shooed me to my seat halfway through the story.

The plastic head had been a gift from my father, and I was only repeating a bedtime story he'd told me. Even then I was marked. His son.

Someone lifted the flap. My father crawled in, his glasses fogged with steam. Had I summoned him? He sat across from me and removed his specs. His eyes, so familiar, looked into mine. "It's hot in here, Perk," he said.

I sprinkled water and the steam rose. He wavered momentarily, then came into focus. Real. He was there.

"I hope I'm not disturbing you. Your mother said you'd be ready to talk now. How do you feel?"

"Disa . . . disassoc . . . crappy. And tired."

"You've done a good job of avoiding me," he said. "You ignored my phone calls. Always too busy to talk. Did you get my letters?"

"Yes."

"Did you read them?"

"No."

"Why, Perk? It's been hard to be in the field and to have lost all contact with my son. Three years without a word."

"You could have come back. Like you did when I was born."

He squinted. There were wrinkles around his eyes

and only a vestige of his hair remained. Time was creeping up on him. "It's not that easy. I was halfway across the world. It takes years to get the trust of a tribe. You can't just give it up."

"What about the trust of a son?"

He bit his lip. "Percy. Perhaps . . . perhaps I should have come home sooner."

"You can have your eyes back."

"What?"

"I can't look through them anymore. I need a break."

I held out my hand, palm up. "Take them."

He still didn't understand, but he moved closer and took my hand. I felt an ache in my eyes. I blinked. My sight sharpened.

"I . . . I . . . I pretended you were dead," I said. "I believed it, in fact."

He furrowed his brow, wrinkling up his forehead. "I—I see."

Time was stretching again. Between us. Sweat trickling down my forehead, down his, too. Like looking in a mirror.

"How was the field?" I asked.

"Long. Tiring. It was my last trip. I'm moving home. To Chicago."

He looked disappointed that he had to admit this. I half expected him to launch into a story the way he had when I was a child, about piranha-infested rivers, giant boas, ancient temples. That wasn't his world now. He would have tenure and an office with a window and a rusty air conditioner that dripped. A home with a green lawn, lawnmower and Cindy Mozkowski.

Things change. They evolve. One has to adapt to these changes.

"It is good to see you again, Dad," I said, "with my own eyes."

"Oh, Perk," he said, "Perk. I'll see you more often now. I promise."

A wisp of steam rose between us. "I hope so, Dad. I do."

epilogue

The next day my father flew home. I borrowed Gray Eyes' car (an ancient Volvo) and drove Dad to the airport. We chatted in the lobby, saying nothing particularly significant to each other.

After he had boarded, I went to the window and watched his plane take off. The airport was small, so it wasn't hard to figure out which one it was. I waved.

When I got home I was tempted to collapse into my bed, but instead I picked up the phone and dialed Elissa's number, my palms sweating. She answered, and in a shaky voice I asked her to meet me at the Broadway Roastery. She agreed.

I arrived early.

"Hi, Percy," she said, strolling in. Her hair was tucked behind her ears. Two skulls dangled from her earlobes. "How's your head?"

I had so many possible answers for that. "Bald but still on my shoulders."

She smiled briefly, then went to the counter and

returned with a cappuccino. "You know, you shouldn't get so wrapped up in things," she said.

I sipped my tea. "Right now I don't want to be wrapped up in anything."

"Good."

An uncomfortable pause followed. It grew longer. We drank from our cups. I began to tell her about the sweat lodge, then stopped.

"I'm sorry I hurt you," I said finally.

She nodded. "Yeah, I know."

"I—I saw my dad."

"Knew that, too. Good."

"How long did you know? That . . . he wasn't dead?"

"Will and I figured it out. We made a pact that we wouldn't ask you. We'd hoped you'd eventually tell us. You must have been very angry with him."

"I was."

People walked by the window, heading to the stores up the street.

"So did the sweat help?" she asked.

"It cleared my sinuses."

She laughed. "Be serious."

"It centered me. I guess."

"Will that be enough?"

I shrugged. "I think I'll call up Mr. Verplaz. Have a talk with him. I'm sure he must get bored in the summer. It'll give him something to do."

"I'm glad to hear that."

Silence. Again. More watching through the window.

"Uh . . . ," I said, "if you have time in the next little while, call me. Maybe we could go to a movie."

"No, Percy."

My heart felt as though someone were squeezing it. Then she said, "You call me. Maybe I'll come." She stood up. "I have to go walk Fang."

We hugged, briefly; then she was gone.

I went home and life returned to normal. I avoided my field journal for the first week of summer. And the second. It loomed too large on my desk, heavy as an obelisk. I refused to turn my television on or open any books. I only used my room for sleeping. I went for walks along the river. My hair began poking out of my skull.

I visited Mr. Verplaz several times, engaging in long discussions about fathers, sons and dream worlds. He even gave me advice on a few university classes and loaned me a couple of jazz CDs, explaining that they'd calm me—they proved that something beautiful could emerge from chaos.

And eventually I convinced myself to phone Elissa.

"So, um, you want to go to a show?"

"Can't," she said. "Why didn't you call before?"

"I—I was busy." I decided to tell her the truth. "And I wasn't ready yet."

"Phone me again at the end of August. Ma and Pa decided to give me a surprise Grad gift. We're jetting off to Rome."

"When?"

"Tomorrow! They want us to have some quality time together. Might kill me. But I could always feed them to the lions in the Colosseum. See ya when I'm back, kiddo."

And so I was left with a lot of time to myself. I read fantasy novels and listened to jazz.

Weeks later a postcard arrived with a statue of Minerva on the front. On the back was written:

> *Hey. They have statues of me here.*
> *Carpe Diem, Perky!*
> *E.*

I laughed out loud.

Finally, on August 6, I opened the journal and flipped through it. There were over seven hundred pages of articles with hundreds of footnotes and a vast number of intricate drawings of skulls and apes and humans. Three years of work. I couldn't quite remember the person who'd written all this; he seemed to have had so much energy. I closed the book. It was still too heavy to move.

I went for a walk and found myself in front of Will's house. I hadn't been there for ages. The curtains in his room were open, and I grinned when I saw that his mother had left his *Planet of the Apes* posters up.

"You really do rock, Will," I said to the ether.

What had I learned? I asked myself as I made my way to the river. I found no clear answer. But I did know this—the sun produces over two hundred trillion trillion trillion neutrinos every second. These tiny particles pass unhindered through space, and through the planets, including Earth. Some are relic neutrinos, left over from the birth of the universe. Billions of neutrinos shoot through our bodies every second on their way back to outer space. For them, it's almost as if we didn't exist at all.

I thought about this as I strolled along the river, sat down on a patch of green grass and felt the sun's rays warm my skin.

So much passes through us without our ever noticing.

.

Arthur Slade (genus and species: *Homo sapiens*) was born in Moose Jaw and raised on a ranch in the Cypress Hills of southwest Saskatchewan, Canada. There he learned how to ride herbivores and drive mechanized farm implements. Early in his development, he began writing; he is the author of five novels for young adults and has won several prizes, including the Governor General's Award for Children's Literature. His current habitat is a house in the mythical city of Saskatoon. Arthur Slade can be visited virtually at www.arthurslade.com.